WICKED LITTLE
Boston's Eli

Tess Summers
Seasons Press LLC

Published: 2022

Published by Seasons Press LLC.

ISBN: 9798371754301

Copyright © 2022, Tess Summers.

Edited by Eden Bradley.

Cover by OliviaProDesign.

This is a work of fiction. The characters, incidents and dialogues in this book are of the author's imagination and are not to be construed as real. Any resemblance to actual events or persons, living or dead, is completely coincidental.

This book is for mature readers. It contains sexually explicit scenes and graphic language that may be considered offensive by some.

All sexually active characters in this work are eighteen years of age or older.

BLURB

It was supposed to be an anonymous, one-night stand.

Dr. Olivia Lacroix wasn't proud that she went to the bar when she was ovulating, intending to get pregnant. No last names or phone numbers had to be exchanged—the guy never needed to know. No harm, no foul. Right?

Wrong.

When her one-night stand shows up at the hospital right after she's given birth demanding answers, he's no longer the nice guy she met in the bar. Not satisfied with her explanation, he insists she marry him or else he's going to sue her for full custody. Olivia has money, but not the kind of money her infant son's father apparently has. She had no idea she'd hooked up with a multi-millionaire.

What else can she do but marry him? Their prenup guarantees her joint custody if *he* divorces *her*. That should be easy enough to make happen. If she can keep from falling in love with the grouch first.

Do you like free books?

Sign up to receive my weekly newsletter, and get your free full-length novel, exclusively for newsletter subscribers! BookHip.com/SNGBXD

She's a badass SWAT rookie, and he's a playboy SWAT captain... who's taming who?

Maddie Monroe

Three things you should not do when you're a rookie, and the only female on the SDPD SWAT Team... 1) Take your hazing personally, 2) Let them see you sweat, and 3) Fall for your captain.

Especially, when your captain is the biggest playboy on the entire police force.

I've managed to follow rules one and two with no problem, but the third one I'm having a little more trouble with. Every time he smiles that sinful smile or folds his muscular arms when explaining a new technique or walks through the station full of swagger... All I can think about is how I'd like to give him my V-card, giftwrapped with a big red bow on it, which is such a bad idea because out of Rules One, Two, and Three, breaking the third one is a sure-fire way to get me kicked off the team and writing parking tickets for the rest of my career.

Apparently, my heart—and other body parts—didn't get the memo.

Craig Baxter

The first time I noticed Maddie Monroe, she was wet and covered in soapy suds as she washed SWAT's armored truck as part of her hazing ritual. I've been hard for her ever since.

I can't sleep with a subordinate—it would be career suicide, and I've worked too damn hard to get where I am today. Come to think of it, so has she, and she'd probably have a lot more to lose.

So, nope, not messing around with Maddie Monroe. There are plenty of women for me to choose from who don't work for me.

Apparently, my heart—and other body parts—didn't get the memo.

Can two hearts—and other body parts—overcome missed memos and find a way to be together without career-ending consequences?

TABLE OF CONTENTS

Wicked Little Secret

PROLOGUE

Olivia

"I'm not really sure what you expect me to say, Liv. You specialize in this—you know your options probably better than I do."

Olivia slumped back in her chair as she looked across the desk at her best friend and business partner.

"I know Rose. I just—I don't know, was hoping I was missing something."

"There are really only two options, my friend. You get knocked up the old-fashioned way—"

Olivia snorted. "Well, since I haven't had sex since Casey Montoya dumped me almost a year ago..."

"Ugh. Inigo the douchebag. You dodged a bullet with that one, babe."

"I know that now. I just wish I wouldn't have wasted three years of my life with him."

"That's on him. He strung you along."

"That's true. But now I'm the one with the expiring biological clock."

Casey had promised her he wanted to get married and have kids; he just wanted to wait until he was promoted. Then he got the promotion and he wanted to wait until he bought a new car, then when he had saved more money. Finally, when she turned thirty-seven and knew her time to get

1

pregnant was running out, she announced she was going off birth control, and he promptly ended their relationship—only to start dating a co-worker ten years his junior a week later. He swore nothing had happened while they'd been together, but Olivia found the timing awfully suspicious.

So, she was back to square one, only this time she was four years older and had no prospects in the baby daddy department.

"Or you go to the sperm bank."

Olivia sighed in resignation. "And pay thousands of dollars for something that might not work."

"Come on, it's not like you're struggling for money."

"And I'd like to keep it that way. If it didn't work the first time, then I'd be invested and would need to keep trying. Then, *poof!* Before I knew it, my savings would be gone. If I'm going to be a single mom, I'm going to need that financial safety net for other things." She rubbed her temples. "I don't know what to do. I'm almost thirty-eight; I don't have a lot of time here."

Rose gave her a sympathetic smile. "When do you ovulate next?"

"I'm ovulating now."

"Well, maybe by next month you'll have met someone."

"Even if I did, I think a month might be a little too soon to suggest having a baby without him running for the hills."

"That's true."

Olivia appreciated her friend at least commiserating with her and trying to think of solutions.

"Have you talked to Scott about a professional courtesy discount? Lord knows we've referred enough patients to him."

She sighed. "He said he'll waive the admin fee, but that's really all he can do without losing money."

Rose grinned. "Maybe pull one of the thoracic guys into the doctor's lounge and do him bareback. Rumor is Dr. Stone is a stallion."

"Yeah, 'cause *that* wouldn't be a problem in about four months when I start to show. And, ew, those guys are whores. I'm pretty sure they wouldn't go without a condom. God, at least I hope not."

Her friend waggled her eyebrows. "Well, you could find out and report back."

"I'll pass." She put her hands on her thighs and announced, "Alright, it's late. I'm going to stop at Flannigan's for some takeout and head home."

Olivia stood up and Rose walked around her desk to accompany her to the door.

"Maybe you should eat there. You're not going to find any potential baby daddies sitting at home."

"I know, but I feel weird going out to eat by myself. I don't want people to think I'm a loser."

"The key is to project confidence, like you own the place. People pick up on your energy. If you act like you don't belong, then that's how they'll treat you. But I'm happy to be your wing woman next time. I just need a little notice to coordinate with Chad's schedule or line up a sitter."

Rose's husband was a sexy cop she'd met when he responded to a fender bender she'd been in. They were married five months later and popping out kids not long after, and Olivia had delivered every one of their babies. Rose had promised to reciprocate when Olivia got pregnant, but she was starting to worry she might never get to cash in on that favor.

Pulling her phone from her white coat pocket, Rose tapped her screen. "Let's plan on a month from now, when you're ovulating next. Chad's off that weekend."

"It's a date."

**

"Evan calling," the robotic voice announced over the speakers in her Mercedes.

She pushed 'answer' and said loudly into the cabin of the sedan, "Hey! What's up?"

"I was just on my way to meet my date and thought I'd give you a call to see how the car is running."

"It's running great." Olivia had bought her brother's old Mercedes a few months ago when he'd wanted the newest model. "Who's the lucky girl?"

"Some chick I met online. We'll probably have one drink and then go get naked."

"Seriously? You're that confident?"

"Yeah. It's kind of implied with the app we're on. Plus, if it wasn't, our conversations have pretty much spelled it out."

"Aren't you worried you're going to get someone who turns into a stalker?"

"A little. Which is why I tell them I'm a stockbroker, and my name is Elliot."

"Oh, for fuck's sake, Evan, seriously?"

"Did you not just hear what I said? *Elliot*," he corrected smugly.

"How can you go home with someone who doesn't even know your real name?"

"First of all, I never go to anyone's home—we always go to a hotel or, a few times, my car, and secondly, you should try it. Sex fixes a lot of things that are ailing you."

It would fix what was ailing her, that was for sure.

He didn't give her time to respond. "It sounds like you're in the car. Are you going out?"

"I am. I just left work. I'm stopping by Flannigan's to pick up something to eat, then I'm headed home."

"Why don't you try picking up a dude while you're there?"

She could practically hear the smirk in his voice.

"I gotta go."

"Love you, Ollie," he sing-songed. He only called her Ollie when he was trying to annoy her.

"Yeah, yeah. Love you, too."

He quickly shouted, "You need to get lai—!" before she clicked off the call.

She did need to get laid.

And pregnant.

Preferably the old-fashioned way, and not artificially inseminated in some exam room at the fertility clinic. She didn't want to go that route; not when all tests indicated she should be able to conceive.

So when she walked into Flannigan's and saw the silver fox sitting at the end of the bar, she decided maybe she wouldn't get her order to go after all.

CHAPTER ONE

Maverick

"Hey Dan," his younger brother called to their bartender as he waited on a pretty blonde at the middle of the bar. "Her drink's on me."

The woman mouthed, "Thank you," and gave a come-fuck-me smile.

Maverick sighed and murmured quietly, "That's the third girl tonight whose drinks you've comped, Derrick."

Derrick pulled the small red straw from his mouth with a grin as he kept his eyes on the woman.

"What's the point of owning a bar if you can't buy a beautiful woman a drink?"

"*Co*-owning a bar. And I don't know... to make money?"

"I'm not sure if you've noticed, but the place is packed," he said as he slid off his barstool. "You're welcome. Excuse me; I need to make sure my customer's *needs* are being met. You should try it. It might make you less grumpy."

Maverick pinched the bridge of his nose. He had no desire to talk to anyone, customer or otherwise. He was a *silent* partner for a reason. While he was skilled at a few things—namely flying jets and making money—his brothers were the ones who had perfected the art of schmoozing.

Which was probably why they had sex a helluva lot more than he did these days.

But Derrick might be on to something. When was the last time he'd even had sex? It'd been a while. Maybe he should try harder to get laid. But as Mav surveyed the crowded bar, none of the younger women appealed to him. He didn't want to be the lecherous old guy hitting on twenty-somethings, and he'd yet to find a match closer to his age that was worthy of a second date on that ridiculous dating app he'd signed up for.

Maverick took comfort in the fact that even though his three younger brothers might be getting their dicks wet a lot more than he was, he made way more money than all of them combined. In addition to investing in each of his younger siblings' businesses in exchange for part ownership of them, he also had an extensive real estate and stock portfolio, plus a few other companies he'd invested in.

His son, Nick, had just pitched him an idea for a lawn care and snowplow business he could do part-time while he finished his degree in landscape architecture and planning. Maverick had pretended to be considering it, but the truth of the matter was, he'd do just about anything for his kids. That Nick had the foresight to come up with the idea and the initiative to make a business plan for it had sold him almost immediately. But still, he needed to play the part of stoic, considerate businessman, so he hadn't said yes—yet.

Derrick, the baby brother of the family, had done almost the same exact thing when he'd had a chance to acquire Flannigan's a few years ago. His business plan for the neighborhood pub trying to emulate the famous Boston bar on television had been spot-on. His brother had been killing it—and Maverick's bank account appreciated it.

While it probably was true that usually you could go to Flannigan's and everybody knew your name, that wasn't the case tonight. The bar was packed for a Tuesday, but every TV in the place showing the Bruins playing in Montreal probably had something to do with that. It didn't hurt the team was in the running to make the playoffs. Derrick's now-empty seat was the only one available in the place.

So how Maverick zeroed in on her in the lobby, he had no idea. But he'd been unable to take his eyes off her from the second she strutted through the door.

He was mesmerized—that was the only reason he could think of why he was taking a play from Derrick's handbook.

Holding out his credit card, he called Dan over.

"You leaving already, Mav?" the man asked as he took his card.

He shook his head. "See that woman who just walked in?"

The bartender turned and looked in the direction of the entrance. "The hottie in the black skirt and pink blouse?"

"Yeah. Everything she orders tonight is on me."

He glanced back at the woman, then again at Maverick. "What if she's meeting someone?"

Shit.

"Hadn't thought about that." He scrubbed his hand across the stubble on his chin.

Dan smirked. "Only one way to find out," he said, then walked to the other end of the bar and loudly yelled, "Miss! Miss!" until he got the raven-haired beauty's attention.

"There's an empty seat at the end of the bar," he boomed as he pointed to the chair next to Maverick.

She nodded her understanding and mouthed, "Thanks," then started walking his way in her black high heels.

Dan turned around with a wicked grin as he walked back to where Maverick was seated. "Now it's up to you, Top Gun."

Even though he hadn't flown a jet for the Navy in almost ten years, his call sign was with him for life. He'd been branded Maverick the first day in flight school when his classmates learned his real name was Pete Mitchell—the main character's name in the Top Gun movie.

He jabbed back with another Tom Cruise movie name. "Thanks, Cocktail."

Dan waved his credit card at him. "Be sure you give me a big tip when you get her digits."

Moments later, a soft voice asked, "Is anyone sitting here?"

"Just you," Maverick replied with his best flirty grin.

She sat down next to him and tucked her long dark hair behind her ear as she glanced at her lap, then quickly pulled her shoulders back and smiled.

Fuck me.

She was even more stunning up close. Her porcelain skin was flawless, with slightly ruddy cheeks, like she was either hot or embarrassed, and her bowtie lips had a tint of pink gloss on them he had a sudden urge to kiss off.

"I completely forgot the game was on tonight," she murmured as she glanced around.

"You forgot? You're not from around here, huh?"

"Oh, no. Born and raised. Other than when I went away to college, I've lived here my whole life. I've just got a lot going on right now and haven't been following the Bruins or the Celtics very closely." She offered a defeated smile that conveyed a lot more than she probably realized as she scanned the room. "I'm guessing they're doing well this season."

He chuckled. "You could say that. But it sounds like you could use a drink, darlin'."

"That," she let out a puff of air, "is an understatement."

Dan appeared and threw a cocktail napkin with the Flannigan's logo in front of her. "What can I get you?"

"Oh, um..." she surveyed the bar patrons' drinks. "Could you make me a dirty martini?"

"One or two olives?"

She gave him a flirty grin and winked. "Could you make it three?"

"Wink at me like that again, and I'll make it a double," Dan flirted back.

While Maverick knew being friendly with customers was part of Dan's job, he still wanted to punch the bartender in the throat.

"As much as I'm tempted to see if you're bluffing, I probably should get some food in me before I do something crazy like that. I haven't eaten since breakfast."

Dan didn't miss a beat as he slid a menu in front of her, then moved to the computer screen a few feet away.

"Oh, I don't need that," she called out to him. "Can you order me a cheeseburger, medium, and fries?"

The bartender tapped some buttons before heading down the bar to put the martini ingredients in a stainless-steel shaker.

Maverick tried to think of something witty to say to this gorgeous woman, but came up empty. No wonder he hadn't had sex in months.

Fortunately, she turned to him and asked, "Are you a big Bruins fan?"

"Isn't everyone this time of year?"

"Apparently not me," she said with a self-deprecating, theatrical sigh before taking a sip from the martini glass Dan had placed in front of her. She set it down and offered her hand. "I'm Olivia, by the way."

"Pete." His large hand dwarfed her petite one. Her fingers were cool from holding the chilled drink glass, but her skin was silky soft. "So, Olivia, what brings you out on a Tuesday night if you weren't planning on watching the game?"

Her lips twitched playfully over the rim of her glass as she took another sip.

"I just got off work and didn't feel like going home yet."

"Overbearing husband?"

She laughed. "No. Nothing like that."

"Demanding kids?"

Her smile fell briefly, but she quickly recovered. Had he not been studying her so closely, he might have missed it.

"Just me and my two cats. But ever since I bought them an automatic feeder, they really have no use for me."

He had a few uses for her, and they all involved her being naked.

"So you don't have to rush home to them."

She looked him dead in the eye. "I could stay out all night if I wanted." After a dramatic pause, she added, "And they wouldn't miss me."

The corner of his mouth hitched, and his dick moved in his jeans. "Good to know." He took a pull from his beer bottle as he looked at the TV and murmured, "I also could stay out all night if I wanted to," then glanced at her for her reaction.

"Oh, my. Think of all the trouble we could get into."

He let his eyes wander over her, resting on her cleavage for a beat. Her nipples poked through the thin fabric of her blouse under his appraisal. He was glad she seemed as affected by him as he was her.

"Why do I get the feeling I'd enjoy getting into trouble with you?" he murmured.

"Because you would."

Her confidence, coupled with how hot she was, now had his cock at almost full mast in his jeans, making his current seating arrangement uncomfortable.

He stood and put his hand in his pocket to subtly adjust himself as he told her, "I'll go check on your order, darlin'."

"It's okay. I'm not in a hurry."

"The sooner you finish your dinner, the sooner we can consider leaving to get into trouble."

Olivia

Was she crazy to actually be considering this? After her conversation with Rose she knew she needed to do something; she just hadn't planned on it happening so soon. But then she'd noticed the gorgeous man the minute she walked in, and it seemed like a sign.

He was almost perfect. Other than maybe being a little older than what she'd envisioned, he was exactly what she was looking for. Actually, he might have been a little too perfect for what she had in mind. When she'd made this crazy plan, she hadn't considered what would happen if she *liked* the guy.

Olivia glanced nervously at Dan, who had been watching her and Pete with amusement as he dried glasses with a bar towel.

"Is he allowed to go back there?"

The man laughed. "They're not going to tell him no."

Before she could ask why not, Pete reappeared and slid back on his barstool.

"It'll be out in a minute."

"Do you make it a habit of going into restaurant kitchens to check on orders?" she teased as she drained her glass.

"The ones I own, yeah."

Olivia fought to keep from choking on her martini and hastily set the empty glass down on the bar as she coughed and tapped her chest. His eyes followed where her hand lay.

"You're the owner?"

"Yeah. Well, one of them."

"So is your last name Flannigan?"

"Noooo," he drew the word out with a laugh. "This place has been here since I was a kid. We just bought it a few years ago."

We just bought it. *Oh god, was he married?* Not that she'd done anything inappropriate—but she'd thought about it.

She blinked at him. "You and your wife?"

That made him burst out laughing as he held up his left hand and wiggled his ring finger, void of any jewelry. "Divorced—going on ten years. I wouldn't suggest getting into trouble with you if I were."

"No?"

"Not my style, darlin'. I'm as faithful as they come."

His admission made her belly strangely warm. "So, who is *we*?"

"This is really my brother's place. I'm just the silent partner."

"The guy with the money."

He gave a modest laugh. "Something like that."

"So, what do you do?"

"I'm retired from the Navy, but I have a few other businesses I'm invested in that keep me out of trouble."

"Wait," she said with a smile. "I thought you wanted to get *into* trouble."

His mouth turned up in a crooked grin she found sexy as hell. "That was only after I met you."

She bit her bottom lip but didn't look away. She was having too much fun flirting with him. Their chemistry was off the charts.

When the bartender had directed her to the seat next to the guy she'd immediately noticed, she thought that had been a sign from the universe. After chatting—okay, flirting—with him, she was more certain about what she was planning. He ticked all her boxes: tall, handsome, appeared fit, nice smile, charismatic, and he was turning out to be an intelligent conversationalist. He was—to quote her favorite nanny—practically perfect in every way, at least for what she had in mind.

"What about you? Where do you work?"

She blurted out without thinking, "Boston General," then winced internally when she thought of her conversation with her brother in the car.

Evan had practically dared her to do this. In fact, she was going to blame her actions tonight on her twin.

What she was considering doing made her a hypocrite in every sense of the word. She'd lost count of the number of times she'd lectured her patients about having unprotected sex with a stranger. But her biological clock wasn't just ticking—it was clanging like cymbals in a marching band.

The handsome man sitting next to her might be the solution she was looking for. She'd get to know him a little better, of course. Maybe try to sneak in a few innocent family history questions, but right now she had every intention of asking him to have unprotected sex with her in the hopes of getting knocked up.

Then never calling him again.

No harm, no foul, right? People—hell, her brother—did it all the time. What Pete never knew wouldn't hurt him. She'd never ask for anything from him. Just his 23 chromosomes tonight.

It seemed like the perfect solution.

The problem was, when she'd begun formulating this idea, she hadn't counted on enjoying his company this much.

But she needed to stick to the game plan, and anonymity was a big part of that. Which was why not revealing too much about herself was probably a good idea. Hence the lie to his next question.

"Oh, what do you do there?"

"I'm an ER nurse."

She knew enough about the emergency room from her brother that she could muddle her way through should Pete want more details.

"That must be stressful."

"It can be. There's never a dull moment, that's for sure."

"It was busy today, huh?"

Aw, crap. Did he actually go to the emergency room earlier? That'd be just her luck to get called out on her first attempt at lying.

"How did you know?"

"You said something about not having eaten since this morning. I figured it was probably because you were busy."

"It's always a madhouse."

He lifted his chin toward the game on TV. "Is that why you don't know we're in the running to make the playoffs? Or why you looked like you needed a drink when you sat down?"

"Well, I'm going to blame work for being out of the hockey loop. But the drink was about other stuff."

"Other stuff." Pete repeated slowly. "Care to talk about it?"

She gave him a flirty smile. "Just needed a little liquid courage to talk with the handsome stranger sitting next to me."

"Coulda fooled me, sweetheart. When you waltzed through the door, the first thing I thought was I'd never seen a more confident woman in my life."

Olivia laughed nervously. "I guess I'm good at faking it."

He pinned her with his stare. "You won't ever have to fake it with me. That I promise you."

She knew damn well he wasn't talking about her projecting confidence, and she believed him that there'd be no need to fake anything if they ended up naked.

He pointed to her empty glass with raised brows. "Do you want another?"

She really shouldn't.

"Maybe one more."

He signaled to Dan, and she gratefully took a sip when the bartender set a fresh one in front of her.

"Do you have kids?"

His blue eyes lit up and he smiled brighter than she'd seen him do all night.

"Two boys. My oldest is a junior at BCU, and my youngest just finished Navy boot camp."

"You must be very proud."

"So fucking proud. They grew up to be amazing young men. While I'd like to think I played a part, I know their mother was a major factor. I was off flying fighter jets while she was raising them. That's my biggest regret in life—not being around more when they were growing up. "

She liked that he was giving props to his ex-wife instead of bad-mouthing her.

"Do you two get along?"

He chuckled. "Yeah—once we got divorced. Not so much at the end of our marriage, though. But she found someone that makes her happy and is a good stepdad to my boys, but still respects that I'm their father, so I got really lucky. We've always presented a united front—rules were the same no matter whose house they were at."

"Wow. That sounds... healthy."

"It was important for our kids, so we sucked it up. Isn't that what a good parent does?"

"You'd think. But in my experience, that's not usually the case."

He winked at her. "Let's not talk about my ex. Or any of yours. Isn't there some unwritten rule about not bringing up past relationships on a first date?"

She smirked. "Yeah, but I didn't know we were on a date."

"With what I'd like to do to you later, darlin', we better be on one."

She took a gulp of her martini as her food was set in front of her.

"Should I be scared?"

"Only if you don't like orgasms."

****

Maverick

He braced himself for a slap across the face.

Sure, she'd been giving him signals since she sat down, but even he knew he might have crossed the line with that remark.

Frankly, it wasn't his style to come on that strong. Once they were naked, sure. But he thought he possessed more finesse than that before actually getting a woman into bed.

So he was elated when, instead of tossing her fresh martini at him, she popped a fry in her mouth and retorted, "On the contrary—I'm a huge fan," without missing a beat.

He leaned closer and murmured in her ear, "Well, you're in luck, because I'm a huge fan of giving them."

Her sharp intake of breath was exactly the reaction he'd been hoping for. Though, you could've knocked him on his ass with what she said next.

"Well, we might have a problem, because I find giving as pleasurable as receiving. Do you think you can keep up?"

Annnd, his cock was hard again.

"I'm an old man, darlin', but I'm not that old. You've got nothing to worry about."

She swallowed her bite of cheeseburger, then took a drink of her martini before responding, "Good to know. You might have to prove it to me."

"That's the plan, sweetheart. That's the plan."

Maverick got Dan's attention and made a motion to indicate he wanted to settle his tab. Seconds later Dan set the charge slip in a black leather-bound bill holder in front of him, along with his card.

"Oh, can I have my check, too?" she asked as she wiped her mouth with her napkin.

Dan tilted his head toward Maverick. "He took care of it for you."

She turned to face him with a smile. "You didn't have to do that."

He shrugged. "I wanted to."

"Thank you. I appreciate it."

Her smile and acknowledgement meant a lot to him. On the handful of dates he'd been on recently, he'd paid each time and found probably half didn't even say thank you. Manners counted a lot to the Salty Dog. His parents had ingrained that in him. And anything they'd missed, the Navy had taken care of.

"It was my pleasure—truly."

They stared at each other for an awkward beat. Then she glanced down and fidgeted with the stem of her martini glass before finally looking up at him through hooded eyes and asking, "So, should we see what kind of trouble we can get into across the street?"

He knew there was a chain hotel kitty-corner from the bar and his heart skipped a beat that this might really be happening—she wasn't all talk.

Offering his hand to help her down off the barstool, he murmured, "I can't think of a better idea."

CHAPTER TWO

Olivia

The second they stepped into the night air, Pete swung her in front of him and held her head as he kissed her on the mouth. She parted her lips without hesitation, happy to discover he was an excellent kisser before things progressed further. When his tongue searched hers out, she instinctively wrapped her arms around his neck. That quickly led to him grabbing a handful of her hair as his kisses became more urgent.

She melted into his body, and yet it felt like she couldn't get close enough to him. Taking her cue, Pete yanked her closer, his thigh positioned between her legs as he pressed her hips against his body while he angled his mouth to deepen the kiss. They only came up for air when another couple exited the restaurant.

Not letting her go, he growled in her ear, "Let's take this across the street."

All Olivia could do was nod her head yes. She was so intoxicated by him that he could have said, 'Let's go play in the street,' and she would have agreed.

She buried her head in his chest and shivered. Alarm bells should be going off in her head with what she was about to do. On paper, it was dangerous, but that was far from how she was feeling. The unusual combination of how turned on, yet how safe he made her feel, was almost overwhelming.

He directed her into the hotel and sat her down in the lobby to wait as he went to the front desk. While sitting there, she was glad she'd had just enough to drink that it allowed her not to overthink what she was doing. As much as she wanted this, now that it was actually happening it would have been easy to have second thoughts. Fortunately, Pete was back and offered her his hand before she gave the idea any more attention.

In the elevator he took her in his embrace and gently kissed her. Searching her face, he quietly assured her as he tucked a lock of hair behind her ear, "Only what you're comfortable with. What happens next is up to you."

When they entered the hotel room, she suddenly felt awkward and shy. How was this going to transpire? Were they just going to get naked and go for it? That seemed like the best option—before she chickened out. She also knew she needed to say the words, since he'd essentially told her in the elevator she was driving this bus.

"I'd really like to have one of those orgasms you were talking about."

Fortunately, he took it from there and pressed her back against the door without hesitation.

"I'd really like to give you one," he whispered in her ear as he traced her jawline with the back of his fingertips. "Or two. Or three. Any time you want me to stop, just say red."

Her body erupted in goosebumps. She doubted she'd be using her safe word with him.

"I'd like to reciprocate." It was her turn to whisper in his ear. "I'm clean, and I'm on the pill."

Please don't say you've been snipped!

"Perfect, because I don't have condoms with me and wasn't sure if I should leave and go get some."

"Mmm, no. I want to feel all of you inside me. Just you."

"I'm also clean, by the way. Did all the tests at my last physical. Didn't want you worrying about that."

"I trust you."

But you shouldn't trust me. Obviously not about not being clean, but she hadn't been on birth control since she'd told Casey she was going off it.

He slowly unbuttoned her blouse with one hand, staring into her eyes as he did.

"I trust you, too."

A pang of guilt hit her square in the stomach. This was so dishonest.

But A) she was horny, and B) she wanted a baby, so those won out. Her guilt could take a hike. She was doing this, and she was going to enjoy it.

He tugged her bra under her boobs and pulled a nipple into his mouth, swirling his tongue before gently biting down. She let out a quick gasp, and he looked up at her with a smile with the pink nub between his teeth.

He sucked it gently, then released it, switching to her other breast and repeating.

Olivia wound her fingers in his short hair to hold him there as she savored his attention.

He released her nipple from between his lips, but kept a hold on her breasts when he stood up straight. She barely came to his shoulder, even in her heels.

"Is your pussy wet for me, pretty girl?"

She knew it was.

Arching her back to push her boobs farther into his hands, she challenged, "Why don't you tell me?"

****

Maverick

The corner of his mouth hitched. This sassy woman. He didn't know what he wanted to do more—fuck her into submission or worship her body all night.

He'd start with worshipping and go from there.

Dropping to his knees, he hiked her skirt to her waist and looped her right leg over his shoulder while he pulled her black satin panties to the side to reveal a glistening wet pussy. His mouth watered as her delicious aroma overtook his senses.

Maverick ran one finger down her wet slit and back up to spread her juices to her clit, then slowly circled her pearl while watching her reaction as he pleasured her.

"It appears you're soaked, darlin'."

She gasped a quick breath before softly moaning her agreement.

Her scent was driving him wild—he needed to taste her or he was going to burst.

Maverick dove into her pussy like a starving man, lapping at her folds as he pumped one finger inside.

"You taste so fucking good," he groaned as pulled the hood of her clit back and plunged back in to give the knot a proper tongue lashing.

"That feels so fucking good," she countered with one hand on his shoulder.

It was his goal to make her come. He was dying to know how sweet her climax would taste, and it became his mission to find out.

Adding a second finger, he increased the pace of his ministrations, moving his tongue faster to match the tempo.

Olivia clutched the back of his head and shamelessly ground her cunt against his face as her moans grew louder.

"That's it, sweetheart. Come on my face. Come all over it. Let me taste you, baby."

Her body went tense, and she began to chant, "Oh god, oh god," while gripping his head tighter with both hands until her little body started spasming, and she lurched forward.

He pinned her in place, not letting up.

"Take it," he commanded, and soon she cried out again as the second climax tore through her.

This time she forcefully pushed his wet face away, not giving him a chance to wring a third from her.

"Oh. My. God," she panted as she quivered against the door.

Maverick lifted her in his arms and carried her to the bed. There, he pulled back the covers and deposited her on the mattress.

"That," she said with her hand on her stomach, "was the most amazing orgasm I've ever had in my life."

He might have puffed his chest out a little at her admission. "I'm not done with you, darlin'."

****

Olivia

He lay beside her, still fully dressed, and leaned down to kiss her. She could taste herself on his lips and tongue, and it only turned her on more.

She liked the way he kissed: he used just enough tongue to be passionate but not so much that she thought she was making out with a St. Bernard.

While Rose had nicknamed Casey Montoya Inigo the douchebag, she'd secretly been calling him Beethoven, after the movie dog—not the composer.

Pulling away from his mouth, she unbuttoned his shirt. She wasn't as skilled as him and had to use two hands, but with every button she opened, she planted a kiss on his warm skin. Each time, he sucked in a deep breath—making her feel like a goddess.

When the last button was finally undone, she sat back and admired him for a small moment. With just the right amount of muscular definition and hair on his chest and stomach, his masculinity was undeniable. He was amazing to look at and touch.

She traced her fingers from his nipples to his waistband as she planted kisses on his stomach, then lowered her hand to fondle and squeeze him over the fabric of his pants. It was a nice bulge, and she was anxious to become better acquainted with it.

When she reached to undo his belt, he grabbed her by the wrist and kissed her fingertips. The look he gave her was pure lust. "You're beautiful," he whispered.

Olivia didn't doubt for a second that he meant it.

"So are you," she murmured and returned to the task at hand: getting his pants off. However, she left his boxer briefs on in order to tease him first.

Mouthing his cock over the black fabric and cupping his balls, she could feel his thick shaft pulsing with need. A small moan escaped her lips when she felt him undo the clasp of her bra and pull the straps to her elbows so her breasts were completely exposed.

Olivia quickly shed the bothersome garment and rubbed her tits against his bare thigh. The hair on his legs was a delicious tease to her nipples.

Freeing his rock-hard dick from the confines of his underwear, she moaned as it bounced in front of her face. Thicker than average, she couldn't wait to feel him inside her.

She circled the tip with her tongue, stroking him gently from the base as she did. Taking his shaft deep in her throat, she was rewarded with a soft groan of, "Fuuuuuck."

She pulled off his length and murmured, "Mmm, that's the plan, baby."

Mindful not to neglect his balls, she lowered herself between his legs to suck and pull his sac between her lips while she kept the rhythm of her hand steady on his cock.

His twitching abs and soft groans were all the encouragement she needed to know she was doing it right.

Feeling adventurous, she let her tongue explore his taint and the outer part of his ass as he tea-bagged her face. His musky smell was so sexy, and she took a deep breath in to savor it before sucking his skin on the way back to his cock.

Once there, Olivia again took him deep in her mouth—this time not letting her lips touch his shaft. When he was fully engulfed, she drew her lips around him and gently sucked as she withdrew him from her lips, circling the head with her tongue before taking him to the base again and holding him there, the tip bobbing against her throat before pulling back again. She took shallow strokes with her mouth while jerking his shaft from the base.

Tasting something sweet and salty, she took that as her cue to stop so she could finally feel him inside her.

She moved to straddle him at the waist. His blue eyes seemed darker as he looked up at her. His body was so muscular and wide that the mere act of putting her legs on the sides of his body opened her pussy.

Holding her hands on his strong, hairy chest for support, Olivia rubbed her slit along his cock, careful to keep him from penetrating her. Twice she acted like she was going to take him inside her, but then wiggled and moved him away from her entrance.

The third time Pete pinned her hips and thrust in. They both moaned in unison when his cock filled her, and she fell forward, her hair fanning his head.

"You fucking feel amazing," he growled in her ear.

Olivia moved rhythmically back and forth on his cock and soon was sitting up straight in order to take him as deep inside as she could.

Her hips ground against his, and she relished the sensation of them totally entwined before falling forward onto his chest. He hugged her tight with his strong arms and fucked her hard and fast.

She wanted to wiggle her body in delight, but he wouldn't let her move an inch as he thrust into her over and over. The sound of his balls slapping against her echoed in her ears as she let go and basked in the carnal pleasure

Loosening his hold, he drew her chin to his face and kissed her, her taste still on his lips.

Sitting up straight, she put her hands on his thighs and fully exposed herself to him. He grinned like he knew what she was after.

As she moved up and down on his cock, he rubbed her clit—slowly at first to match her rhythm as she seductively rode him. But as she bucked against him harder and faster, the speed and pressure of his fingers increased. She could feel how wet she was, her body humming with need that only his thick shaft could fill. Her nipples stood at full attention while she arched her back and moaned before she started to tense.

The orgasm seemed to hit her out of the blue. The muscles that she'd been holding so tight were suddenly Jell-O as her body relaxed all at once, and she shivered with pleasure.

Before she could even come down from her orgasmic high, Pete flipped her over and plunged his cock in deep. The sensation only served to extend her pleasure.

When he started to grunt, she knew he was about to explode and implored him not to stop.

"Fill me with your cum!"

That was the whole reason she was there.

CHAPTER THREE

Olivia

She sat at her office desk staring at her computer screen. The email with the heading that read 'lab results—Lacroix, Olivia' blinked at her.

In her heart, she knew what it was going to say, but that little sliver of doubt crept into her head, telling her that her symptoms were psychosomatic and nothing more than wishful thinking.

Her hand shook as she clicked 'open' and she quickly scanned the report. It looked like the dozen she reviewed every day, so she knew exactly where to focus.

And there it was in big bold letters—POSITIVE.

Olivia was pregnant.

Slumping back in her chair, she covered her mouth with the tips of her quivering fingers as it sunk in.

I'm going to be a mom.

She thought about the night she'd gotten pregnant. Pete had been such a good guy, and a pang of guilt hit her. She remembered how many orgasms he'd wrung from her before he came a second time and fell asleep, content that he'd satisfied her. And how she'd snuck out instead of allowing herself to snuggle next to him like she'd wanted to.

What she'd done was shitty, and she knew it.

But she was going to have a baby! And that made it worth it. Maybe it was Machiavellian of her, but in her mind, the end justified the means.

She decided to wait before telling anyone.

That decision lasted all of thirty minutes before she was on her way down to the ER to see her brother. She needed to share the news or she was going to burst—and her twin was the first person she thought of.

They'd just talked last night when she went to pick up a pizza. The pizza she threw up an hour later—the reason she decided to take a test when she got to work today.

I swear to God, if he judges me, she thought as she waited for the elevator. Especially after what he told her last night.

The song she had been singing along with on the radio had stopped, replaced with the voice that declared, *Evan calling*.

"Hey! How's my favorite brother?"

"Hey little sister!"

"You'd think after thirty-eight years you'd want to forget about that one minute and let me just be your sister."

"Never!"

The sound of his deep laugh filled the car, and it made her smile. She and Evan had that twin connection, even to this day. They were also highly competitive, which had served them both well throughout the years. Trying to outdo each other had gotten them both into one of the best med schools in the country, where they'd vied to be the top of their class, only to be beaten out by a guy in their study group. They'd gone their separate ways for their residencies, but ended up back together in Boston to practice their specialties.

But he, hands down, had the better social life.

"To what do I owe the pleasure?" she asked.

"Just checking in. I haven't talked to you in a while."

"Pretty sad, considering we work at the same hospital."

"I know, but my hours are a lot more sporadic than yours."

That was true. The ER was short-staffed and her brother didn't have a set schedule.

"Are you on your way to work?"

"Nah, I got a hot date."

Olivia laughed. "Provided you're not being catfished."

"We video chatted. I won't make that mistake again."

"Oh my god," she said as she pulled into the pizzeria's parking lot; the smell of food wafting into her car making her mouth water. "Are you ever going to find someone and settle down?"

"Are you?" he shot back.

"I'd love to, but I need to find the right guy first."

She didn't mention the great guy she'd met a few weeks ago. Or the dirty, dirty things they'd done before she slunk out in the middle of the night while he lay sleeping.

"And if I ever meet the right woman, I'll consider it. In the meantime, this works. I don't want a relationship right now, but I do want sex. You should try it."

She bit her tongue. *I have tried it, thank you very much. And we didn't use a condom.* She'd kick Evan's ass if he ever told her something like that.

"But with some rando, E?"

"Believe it or not, I don't bang just anyone. I am somewhat selective. And the women seem to dig it. I think they find the anonymity liberating so they can get their hidden freak on."

She thought back to her night with Pete. Knowing she wasn't going to see him again had made her a lot more uninhibited. She'd allowed herself to be much bolder than she normally would be.

"Just be careful."

"Always."

Now she was on her way to tell him she was pregnant. Olivia knew he'd take his cues from her, and once he saw that she was happy, would be thrilled for her. But he was going to have a lot of questions. Ones she wasn't sure how she was going to answer.

Maybe she wasn't ready to tell him after all.

After peeking her head into his office and finding his desk empty, she decided that was the universe's way of telling her to wait.

"Hey Liv!" Steven Ericson called as they walked toward each other in the wide hall. "What are you doing down here?"

Steve was another ER doctor and a friend of her brother's. He was California handsome and had always been kind to her whenever they interacted, almost like a second brother.

"I was just looking for Evan. I need to tell him—" and she burst into tears as the words, 'I'm pregnant' went through her head. She really was going to have a baby.

The idea elated her and scared her shitless at the same time.

"Hey," he said, pulling her in for a long hug. He smelled nice—his cologne was a subtle woodsy scent and his arms were strong and protective. After a minute of crying as her emotions bounced all over the place, she took a deep breath and smiled up at him. He returned the smile and kissed her forehead, almost exactly like Evan would do if he were there.

"Come on into my office and tell me what's going on."

She sat in the visitor's chair and blurted out, "I'm pregnant. I just found out about an hour ago."

His face remained blank, like he wasn't sure how he was supposed to react, so she added, "And I'm really excited."

He broke out into a big smile. "That's wonderful. Congratulations! You came down to tell Ev?"

"Yeah, but I'm scared he's going to go all big brother on me and ask a million questions about the father."

"You're not with the father?"

"Not anymore."

She didn't want to sound like the slut she obviously really was.

"So you're going to be a single mom," he observed.

Olivia nodded her head and repeated, "I am going to be a single mom."

She'd planned on that since Casey broke up with her, but saying it out loud felt overwhelming, and she teared up again.

Steve came around his desk and grabbed her hands as he knelt in front of her.

"You're going to be amazing at it. And you have an incredible family and friends to support you. I know Evan will be a terrific uncle, and I'm here to help if you need anything."

She hugged him again. "Thank you."

"Anytime."

He stood up straight, and she got to her feet to let him walk her to the door. She wiped her eyes before opening it, and he hugged her around her shoulders again.

"I mean it—you need anything, call me. But you know Evan will always have your back."

"I know."

While her twin was her biggest competitor, he was also her biggest supporter. The realization of how lucky she was made her start crying again as she walked out the door.

It was going to be a long eight months if she was to cry over the slightest little thing.

Evan was walking down the hall when he saw her come out of Steven's office. His face immediately became alarmed when he saw she was crying.

He quickly approached and grabbed her elbow. "Olivia? What's wrong?"

"Nothing," she said, smiling through her tears.

"Bullshit. Why are you crying?"

It must have been the pregnancy brain that made her blurt out, "I'm going to have a baby."

Her brother's eyes grew wide. "You're what?"

"I'm pregnant. You're going to be an uncle."

She watched him morph into protective older brother right in front of her eyes as he scrubbed his hand across his chin.

"Wh-what? How? Who?"

"Let's go in your office."

She knew that, like Steven, Evan needed some guidance from her as to how to feel about this.

For a second she thought about telling him she'd gone to a fertility clinic, but had the foresight to know that lie would potentially bite her in the ass.

"First of all," she said as she sat down, "I'm thrilled. This is a good thing."

Her brother perched on the corner of his desk. "Who's the father?"

Olivia shook her head. "It doesn't matter." She wasn't sure what compelled her to add, "He doesn't want anything to do with us."

"He *what*?"

Steam practically shot out Evan's ears as he jumped to his feet to pace his office, and she quickly realized that'd been the wrong thing to say.

"It's fine, E. It's better this way."

"Livi—the fuck it is. He—"

She cut him off. "I don't want to talk about him. Period. End of story. *I'm* having a baby, and we're not talking about the father. Ever."

He studied her face for a beat, and she could see his wheels turning as he sized up how serious she was about her edict. She must have looked pretty damn stern because he nodded slowly and said, "Okay. I won't bring it up again."

Dropping on his knee next to her, similar to how Steven had, he caressed her biceps. "I'm here for you and that little peanut. You're not alone in this."

Her bottom lip trembled with how much love he was directing at her.

"I know."

He grabbed her around the shoulders and pulled her in for a hug. "I love you, little sis."

"I love you, too." She let out a big sigh. "I should probably get back to work."

They walked toward his door, and he asked, "Do Mom and Dad know?"

"I don't think I'm going to tell anyone until I make it through the first trimester."

"My lips are sealed, then. You let me know when it's safe to say something around them."

Olivia stood on her tiptoes and pecked him on the cheek. "I will. Thank you. I mean it."

She could tell he wanted to say more, but he just smiled and said, "Of course. That's what big brothers are for."

**

"Shut the front door!" Rose exclaimed a week later when Olivia casually broke the news to her.

"It's true—I have the test results to prove it. I'm finally cashing in the favor."

"Ok, so spill. Did you end up going to the fertility clinic? I thought you didn't want to do that because even with a professional discount, you thought it'd end up being hella expensive."

Olivia took a deep breath. When it came to this baby she was turning into a liar, and it wasn't getting easier with each lie she told. But she was so ashamed of what she'd done to get pregnant that she couldn't even tell her best friend how it really happened. So, she fudged a little.

"I'd been seeing someone casually, and we might have forgotten to use protection one night."

It was *kind of* true.

"Does he know?"

"Um..."

"Olivia Lacroix!" her friend gasped. "You have to tell him!"

"Why?"

"What if he wants to be a part of this baby's life?"

"Yeah—exactly. Then I have to be accommodating, and I don't know if I want to do that. What if he turns into another Casey?"

"So what, you're just going to ghost this guy?"

"No. I'm just not going to be available when he wants to get together. He'll give up and move on. It's not like we had this great romance or anything."

Another pang—right to her heart—as she uttered the words. Because she could imagine having had a great romance with Pete. He'd been kind and considerate, yet just bossy enough in the bedroom, that it was easy to envision what that could have looked like long term.

But she'd tricked him, and she didn't imagine he'd forgive her for that. He seemed too honorable. Must be that military background.

"Don't you think he has a right to know he has a baby on the way?"

Even with how little she knew Pete, she knew he would not be pleased knowing he had a child in the world that was going to know nothing about him.

The thought made her tear up, and her friend, noticing her watery eyes, quickly backtracked.

"If you think it's best, I support you a hundred percent.

"I don't know if it's best," she said through her tears. "I just know it's what I have to do."

"I got your back, girl. Now, let's get your ultrasound scheduled."

CHAPTER FOUR

Maverick

"How was your date last weekend?" Derrick asked when he stopped into Flannigan's for a drink and dinner.

"A fucking disaster. I don't know why I'm even on that dating app. I just need to meet a woman the old-fashioned way."

The devil on his shoulder snorted. *Yeah, cuz that'd worked out so well last time.*

Actually, it had gone great. It was just the waking up and finding her gone with no way of contacting her that had sucked.

He'd been coming back to the bar every Tuesday night for the last four months hoping to run into her again. Of course, he never told his brother that was why.

Derrick chuckled. "So, it's safe to say you're not asking her to the lake for the Fourth then."

Their parents had rented a six thousand square foot 'cabin' in the Catskills on a lake for two weeks, so he and his brothers were spending the holiday weekend there with them.

"More like hiding from her. I tried being polite at the end of the night. Shook her hand, didn't even hug her, and wished her well. I thought I made it pretty obvious I wasn't interested in a second date. I mean, she has a PhD; I didn't think I needed to spell it out for her. But she hasn't stopped texting me, and when I didn't respond she freaking private messaged me on social media!" He shook his head. "I'm not cut out for this shit."

"I'm sorry, man. It's rough out there. But the first thing you need to do is change your social media to Maverick instead of Pete—"

"It already is."

"Or stop telling women your real name."

"Or just stop dating altogether."

"Nah, you're not a quitter," his brother replied with a grin as he wiped the bar in front of Maverick. "The right woman's out there. You'll find her."

Yeah, provided she doesn't sneak out in the middle of the night never to be heard from again.

He made a noncommittal noise, and Derrick asked, "So, just you for the Fourth, then?"

"Yeah. Nick is going to the Cape with friends, and the Navy won't give Nash enough time yet to come home."

"How's he liking Accession Training?"

"I think he likes it. The Florida heat is kicking his ass a little right now, but the girls in bikinis on Pensacola's beaches are helping ease his pain."

Derrick chuckled. "He's doing the Mitchell name proud. Gabe is bringing someone he's been dating; mom's excited."

"Is he bringing the kids, too?"

"No, it's Becky's weekend with them. He doesn't dare ask her to switch."

Their brother had gone through a messy divorce a few years ago. It hadn't been as amicable as Maverick and Patricia's had been.

"What about Beau? Is he bringing someone?"

His brother's mouth hitched in a sly smile. "I don't think so."

"What are you grinning about?"

"I might be bringing someone. Maybe. We'll see how this weekend goes before I ask her."

"Oh yeah? Where'd you meet her?" He didn't even pause to let him respond. "Let me guess, you bought her a drink here one night."

Derrick shrugged. "It worked—you should try it."

He had tried it, and it had succeeded epically—until it hadn't.

Apparently Dan had never ratted him out when he'd paid Olivia's tab. Maybe it was because he'd actually *paid*— including a tip—and not comped it, like his brother had a tendency to do.

"Not my style, you know that."

"You got any more dates lined up from that app you're using?"

"Unfortunately, this weekend. But I think I'm going to cancel. I'm just not up for another night of mind-numbing conversation, and this last one has me nervous."

"Have her meet you here. Somebody can save you if it's going bad. Just send a text, and we'll suddenly have a kitchen emergency. Or Connie can pretend she's your wife or something."

Oh, the fucking drama just to go on a date these days.

"Yeah, maybe. If I go through with it that's probably what I'll do."

Derrick shot Maverick a grin as he slid a draft in front of him. "I'm here for ya, big brother. Don't forget to tip your bartender."

CHAPTER FIVE

Olivia

She lay on the table wearing the hospital-provided gown and stared at the ceiling as her friend waved the wand over her goo-covered belly.

"Okay, moment of truth. Do you want to you know what you're having?" Rose asked.

"Yeah, I decided I do."

Rose put her hand on the monitor but didn't turn it. "Are you sure?"

Olivia took a deep breath. "Yes, I'm sure. But I don't want anyone else to know, so when my brother comes nosing around, you tell him I decided not to find out."

"You got it."

The monitor flipped and Olivia studied it for a minute before breaking into a huge smile when she saw the certain anatomical part.

"A boy," she whispered as tears welled in her eyes.

"Congratulations, mama," her friend said softly as she gripped her hand and squeezed.

"Thanks."

Rose handed her paper towels to wipe her stomach, then said, "I'll let you get changed."

As Olivia cleaned up and put her street clothes on, she contemplated what it was going to be like to have a boy. Was she equipped to parent a boy alone?

Rose had two boys and two girls, so when Olivia walked in her friend's office after she got dressed, she casually asked, "How much does Chad do when it comes to Theo and Connor?"

Her friend tilted her head. "What do you mean? We're both involved with raising the kids, you know that."

"I know. I just mean, like are there things that you let him handle because he's their dad?"

Rose thought about it for a second. "I suppose I defer most penis-related things to him, and he relies on me to handle anything dealing with female parts for the girls. And I appreciate that he models how to be a good man—for all the kids. The girls know how they should expect to be treated by a man, and the boys know what it means to be an honorable man."

Olivia felt the lump in her throat as she nodded. "That's what I thought."

"Why?"

"I'm just wondering if I'm going to handicap my kid if he doesn't have a father to do those things."

"Oh, Liv. No. You're going to love that little boy enough for two parents."

"I know, but what about things I can't teach him?"

"You'll have your dad and your brother as role models."

She snorted. "I'm not sure I want my son emulating Evan."

That made Rose smile. "I know you're just joking. Evan is a good man. A pain in the ass sometimes, but he's a good man."

"I think his daddy is, too," she whispered as she rubbed her belly absent-mindedly. She looked up at Rose as the first tear rolled down her cheek. "Am I making a mistake keeping this from him?"

"Only you can answer that."

"I think I need to tell him."

Rose lifted her shoulders. "So, tell him.

**

She took a deep breath as she opened the heavy wooden door leading to Flannigan's. The parking lot was less crowded than the last time she'd been there months ago, so she wasn't surprised to see plenty of open tables and seats at the bar.

Olivia was leaving for the Cape the next morning to celebrate the Fourth of July. One of the neuros she worked with owned a place right on the beach that he rented out and had a last-minute cancellation, so she decided to spend the next two weeks with her toes in the sand.

But first, she needed to find out how to get a hold of Pete. The bar where they'd met and that he said he co-owned seemed like the most logical place to start. In fact, short of hiring a private investigator, it was the only place she knew to start. And the idea of hiring a PI to track down her one-night stand felt icky.

Her top was flowing, so it was impossible to tell if she was just chubby or pregnant. She'd worn it by design. She wanted to be the one to tell Pete about the baby, not some gossipy bartender.

She didn't recognize the man who set the napkin down in front of her. It wasn't Dan, the man tending bar the night she'd met Pete.

"What'll you have?"

"Can I have a cheeseburger and fries, and a Sprite?"

He flashed her a smile. "You got it," he said, then put ice in a glass and shot a clear liquid from the bar gun into it before handing it to her.

As he walked away, she interjected, "Um, is Pete around by any chance?"

The man turned around slowly. "I'm sorry—who?"

Her first thought was she'd gotten his name wrong. It had been four and a half months, and she had pregnancy brain, so her automatic reaction these days was that she was mistaken.

"Um, Pete? He's one of the owners?"

"I've worked here for almost two years, and I don't know a Pete who's an owner."

Olivia nervously tucked her hair behind her ear. "He's a little older? Dark hair, but grey at the temples? He was in the Navy?"

"You mean Maverick?"

"Uh—Maverick?" She replayed the conversation they'd had in her head. "No, I'm sure he said his name is Pete."

Another man walked behind the bar carrying a rack of glasses.

"Derrick, this lady is looking for someone named Pete?"

Derrick glanced over at her and shook his head, sticking out his bottom lip while shaking his head. "Pete?"

"I think she's talking about Mav," the original bartender offered as he stood punching buttons on a computer screen.

The other man started putting the glasses away, scowling at her as he did. "What do you need him for?"

"Well, um, if they're the same man, he and I went out a while back. I just need to talk to him."

"You went out—but you don't know his name?"

Her spine stiffened. She didn't appreciate the attitude. "He said his name was Pete," she grumbled. "And that he co-owned this place."

His smile was condescending. "I co-own this place. I think maybe you were conned, sweetheart."

Was she? She didn't think so.

She pursed her lips. "Well, the bartender that night seemed to know him. And he went back into the kitchen, and he paid my tab."

Derrick snorted. "Sounds like you dated a waiter."

She glared back at the man, but didn't reply. It felt like anything she did say, he was just going to scorn.

He sighed. "Look, Maverick, Pete, whoever. Like you said, we might not even be talking about the same person, but I haven't seen Mav in weeks, and I have no idea when he'll be in next—he doesn't have a set schedule. It seems like you'd know that if you'd really gone out."

If he was trying to make her feel small—and she suspected that was exactly his objective—he was succeeding.

Still, she'd come here to find Pete and tell him about the baby. She had to at least try to find a way to get in touch with him, despite this jerk.

She took her business card from her purse and wrote her personal cell phone number on the back, then slid it across the bar. "Well, when he comes in next, would you please ask him to call me? It really is important."

The first bartender took the card and handed it to Derrick, who barely glanced at it before sticking it in his shirt pocket. "Will do," he said as he walked away.

She didn't feel confident.

A woman in a server uniform set her plate of food in front of her with a smile. Olivia had suddenly lost her appetite.

"Would you mind bringing me a to-go box?"

She set her credit card on the bar, signaling she wanted her check.

The bartender quickly retrieved it and seconds later, set her receipt in front of her with a smile that seemed forced.

As she hovered over the tip amount, she wavered between a penny for making her feel embarrassed and overtipping, with the hope he'd help her.

She decided on the latter and handed him the merchant copy with a fifty percent tip and her phone number written on it.

"It really is important that I talk to Pete. Can you please make sure he calls me?"

He didn't even look at the receipt, just gave her a dismissive nod. "Yeah, sure."

Dick. Now she wished she had stiffed him.

****

Maverick

It was Tuesday night, so that meant he was having dinner at Flannigan's—something he did almost every week, despite Olivia never showing up again. A guy could hope.

"When are you heading to New York?" Derrick asked as he pulled a draft from the tap and handed it to Maverick.

"Thursday morning. What about you?"

"Probably the same."

"So are you bringing someone?"

"Nah. We went out and I quickly realized I could not spend a long weekend with her."

Maverick chuckled. "I wish I could say I was surprised."

"Yeah, my luck with dating lately seems to be as good as yours. Speaking of... did you block that doctor chick's phone number? The one who was stalking your social media?"

He cocked his head. "Janice? The woman with the PhD?"

"Yeah, her."

"How did you know I blocked her?"

"'Cuz she showed up here last night."

Maverick let out a groan. "You're kidding. How did you know it was her?"

"She asked for 'Pete,' and said you two had gone out, so I was immediately suspicious. Then she left her business card. Doctor someone, so then I knew."

"What'd you tell her?"

"I acted like I didn't know who she was talking about. Except numbnuts," he jerked his head toward Tyler, the younger bartender at the other end of the bar, "asked her if she was talking about Maverick after she described you. It took him a second to catch on that we were playing dumb."

"Fuck," he grumbled, shaking his head.

"You must have given her some good D to have her come looking for you in person," Derrick said with a shit-eating grin.

"I didn't sleep with her. Hell, I didn't even hug her!"

He hadn't slept with anyone since Olivia, the gorgeous ER nurse.

"Well, it's probably a good thing you're getting out of town, then."

Indeed.

CHAPTER SIX

Olivia

A blast of chilly autumn air greeted her when she opened the door for the delivery driver. The Halloween skeleton hanging from her door rattled in the wind.

"I have five boxes on the truck," he said as he eyed her visibly pregnant belly. "I can bring them as far as your entryway."

It was the baby furniture she'd ordered. There was no way she was going to be able to drag the boxes upstairs by herself.

"Can you put them in the garage?" She had an empty stall she could keep them in until Evan came over and put things together.

"Even better, that way I won't trip over your decorations," he quipped as he glanced down at the uncarved pumpkins on her porch.

After the driver left, Olivia surveyed the cardboard boxes with a sigh. She was a strong, independent woman, and she hated having to ask other people for help.

Some leaves blew in the garage with a gust of wind, so she clicked the garage door button closed before she went inside. She had at least another six weeks to worry about the furniture; she'd deal with it later. Right now, she was going to look for the lawn service flyer that had been on her windshield when she'd left the grocery store.

Just one more thing she couldn't do herself.

She'd ended up working on Halloween and missed the trick-or-treaters. It was probably for the best—the last thing she needed was to spike her blood sugar by sneaking candy that was supposed to be for the little witches and goblins. And she inevitably would. Her cravings had been out of control lately.

She'd had a pity party meltdown the night before when she had a specific craving for a Popeye's chicken sandwich and her food delivery driver brought the wrong thing. It had been late, and she hadn't wanted to go out, so when she opened the delivery app and smugly placed her order, she'd felt pretty proud of herself.

"I don't need a partner. I have a smart phone and a credit card."

Then when she pulled out a sandwich she hadn't ordered and fries instead of mashed potatoes, she broke down crying. She couldn't even get the delivery driver—someone she was paying—to take care of her.

Her life was pathetic.

Evan had gotten hot and heavy with Steven's little sister and had been blowing off putting the baby furniture together. Her financial planner never seemed to be in the office when she called about being able to afford taking unpaid time off once the baby came, and the temp agency she and Rose were working with to find her replacement doctor was being vague about the candidates.

With Thanksgiving right around the corner, it was starting to stress her out. Olivia needed to have all her ducks in a row, all the time. This baby was going to be here before she knew it, and she wanted everything shored up *now*.

The only person who'd come through when he said he would was the college kid taking care of her lawn.

He'd shown up on time and raked her leaves, then offered his snowplowing services, which she immediately took him up on.

"You'll be my first customer when we get snow," he assured her when she made a point of telling him she was due the beginning of December.

"Thanks." One less thing for her to worry about.

**

Less than a month later, she paced the floor as she watched the weather report. Of course there'd be a blizzard on her due date.

She'd warned Evan not to go to Hope's bed and breakfast on the Cape, but he wouldn't listen.

"Mercedes is a German car, it's built to handle the snow. I'll be able to get back with no problem if you go into labor."

Olivia looked out the living room window to see the snow starting to pile up on her back patio. The only vehicle that would be able to handle the accumulation they were expected to get was a snowplow.

Maybe the weather gods would be in her favor.

Early the next morning, she woke up thinking she'd peed the bed, only to quickly realize her water broke.

"Oh no," she cried as she rushed to her bedroom window and saw the drifts of snow in her driveway.

It looked like the city snowplow had come through already, so if she could just get her car out of the driveway...

She took a deep breath to calm her nerves.

First things first, get out of her wet pajamas and grab a quick shower.

She'd showered, dressed, and made sure her hospital bag was ready when the first contraction pain hit.

"No! No. No. No."

Nick hadn't shown up to plow her driveway yet, even though he promised she'd be first on his route.

She was looking through the scraps of paper on her desk for his number when she thought she heard his truck in the drive.

Grabbing her coat and slipping on her boots, she opened the garage door. Sure enough, there he was, and she ran outside.

He rolled down his window with a smile.

"Hi," she said as calmly as she could. "Would you mind just plowing behind my car? I need to get to the hospital. I'm, um, in labor."

The young man's eyes got as big as saucers, and he threw open the driver's door.

"What? You're in labor? You can't drive yourself to the hospital!"

"Well, I don't want to wait for an ambulance. I'm not sure what the rest of the roads are like, so who knows when they'd get here."

He grabbed her by the elbow and escorted her to the passenger side.

"I'll take you."

"I need to get my purse and hospital bag, and close my garage door," she argued just as another contraction hit, and she gripped her stomach as she bent forward.

"I'll take care of that. Just tell me where they are."

Nick opened the door and helped her into the truck.

"They're right inside my house, through the door from the garage."

"What's your garage code?"

She told him, and minutes later she watched her garage door come down as he hurried to the truck holding her red weekender bag and black purse.

What a sweet kid.

Hopefully they made it to the hospital in time, and she didn't traumatize him by making him pull to the side of the road and deliver this baby.

CHAPTER SEVEN

Maverick

He pulled his boots on when he heard Nick's truck outside.

Except it wasn't Nick, or Nick's truck that was plowing his driveway, it was his son's friend, Chris. Nick had hired him to help when he was backed up. But no matter how busy he was, Nick always made sure he personally plowed his dad's driveway, so Maverick immediately became concerned.

"Where's Nick?" he asked when Chris stopped and rolled his window down.

"He's at the hospital."

Maverick's stomach immediately dropped to his boots, but he managed to calmly ask, "Is he okay?"

"Yeah. One of his customers went into labor. He was worried the ambulance might get stuck in the snow, so he took her himself."

That sounded like something his son would do.

"Oh, wow. So, you're doing his route?"

"Yeah. It worked out since the place I bartend decided not to open today."

He made a mental note to talk to Derrick about hiring Chris.

"You need any coffee or anything?"

The younger man held up a stainless-steel thermos with a grin. "I'm all set."

Maverick waved and headed back inside the house, dialing Nick's phone the second the door closed.

After the third ring, he was greeted with an enthusiastic, "Hey Dad!"

"Hey buddy! Chris is here plowing my driveway. He said something about you playing ambulance driver?"

"Yeah, one of my customers is pregnant and she came out of her garage in a panic, asking me to hurry so she could get to the hospital because she was in labor. She was actually going to drive herself; can you believe that?"

"Where was her husband?"

"She's not married. And then none of her family or friends could get here in time, so I stayed at the hospital with her. Now I'm an honorary uncle! I'm going to send you a picture! Mom says he looks just like me when I was a baby. Tell me what you think."

Maverick's phone dinged with the incoming text, and he put the call on speaker as he opened up Nick's text message.

There was his son, posing next to the new mother in her hospital bed with the tiny baby, almost like a father would.

Except, Maverick should be the one in the picture.

His heart started beating out of his chest. Nick wasn't the kid's honorary uncle—he was his brother.

He coughed to try to steady his voice before asking, "What hospital are you at?"

"Boston General. I wanted to take her to Banner Hospital, since it was closer, but she insisted I bring her here. I guess this is where she works."

It really is her.

"I'll be there soon."

He ended the call and sat down on the bench in his entryway with a *thunk*.

His beautiful one-night stand, the one he hadn't stopped thinking about for nine fucking months, just gave birth to his baby. He'd bet his life savings the kid was his. He looked just like his boys had when they were born, and the timing was right.

And his son was the one who drove her to the hospital. What kind of cosmic fuckery was that? He'd been looking for this woman for the last nine months, and Nick ended up being the one holding her hand when she gave birth.

That was some divine intervention if he'd ever seen it. And he wasn't going to snub the universe giving him another chance. With her, or at being a dad.

His only question was—why hadn't she told him?

Chapter Eight

Olivia

She stared down in awe at her son as he nestled against her chest. He was tiny perfection. It was scary how much she already loved him.

"He's got a lot of hair," Nick observed when he walked back in the room after taking a phone call.

She smiled at the poor college kid she'd hired to plow her driveway in the winter and take care of her yard during the non-snowy months. He'd been polite every time they'd interacted, but today he'd gone way above and beyond.

"Thank you again for bringing me to the hospital."

He laughed. "I can't believe you really thought you were going to drive yourself."

"I was desperate—and determined. Not always a good combination."

"I'm glad I showed up when I did."

She glanced down at her baby boy. "Me, too. I can't thank you enough. I'm sorry if I've scarred you for life."

"No way; that was the most amazing thing I've ever been a part of!"

"You were a godsend. This blizzard really threw a wrench in my birth plan, that's for sure. I never would have imagined my birth coach getting snowed in and not able to get here."

"Just make sure I'm his favorite uncle—even if I'm only an honorary one."

She chuckled as she imagined her brother's reaction if he heard that. Just then, her phone pinged with a text, and she glanced at the screen. "Speaking of uncles, my brother is on his way. You really don't have to stay. I'm sure you've got other things you need to do."

"Actually, that was my dad who called. I told him what happened, and he's on his way. I hope that's okay."

"Of course." She'd love to meet the man who'd raised such a great kid.

The nurse appeared in the doorway. "How's everything going, Dr. Lacroix? Have you tried nursing him yet?"

Olivia kissed the baby's soft dark hair. Nick was right— he did have a lot of it.

"Not yet."

She hadn't wanted to whip her boob out in front of Nick—she'd traumatized the poor kid enough. He'd kept his head above her waist, so he hadn't been subjected to *that*, but her yelling and squeezing his hand had been plenty.

As if sensing why she was hesitating, he said, "I'll wait in the hall for my dad and give you some privacy."

"Thanks."

It only took a few tries before her son latched onto her nipple, and the nurse left her alone to breastfeed.

Olivia had so much love for this little person in her arms, yet she couldn't help feel a twinge of sadness. She was going to raise him by herself. What if she fucked it up epically? What the hell did she know about boys? Sure, she could treat them for whatever ailed them, but what about the emotional stuff?

Yeah, her brother said he'd help her, along with her friends and parents, but she'd had to throw a temper tantrum before she could even get Evan to put the baby furniture together.

The fact that she'd had to rely on an almost complete stranger to hold her hand while her child came into the world just emphasized that keeping this little boy alive and well-adjusted was going to fall on her, and her alone.

And that was scary as shit.

She took a deep, calming breath through her nose and closed her eyes as she slowly released it.

I am a badass doctor. I can do anything I put my mind to.

Except what was going to happen when she had to go back to work? Then what? What if something happened while he was at daycare?

Ohmygod—someone else is going to raise my child!

A sense of panic crept through her. She'd had a few of these moments since finding out she was pregnant, but they usually passed quickly. She wasn't afraid of being a mom—it'd been what she'd wanted for years, but she was scared of messing up royally. And once again, she wondered if she'd made a mistake getting pregnant without having a husband.

Olivia thought about how much she relied on collaborating with her business partner, Rose, when making important decisions for their practice. And that was just for her business. How was she supposed to raise a tiny *human* alone without screwing up?

She gently stroked his little cheek as she watched him take nourishment from her breast.

"It's you and me, kid," she whispered. "I promise I will always protect you if you promise to forgive me when I mess up along the way."

****

Maverick

He stood quietly in the doorway, watching the intimate moment between a mother and her child.

The love she felt for her newborn was obvious, and had he been observing the exchange between anyone else, he would have felt like he was intruding.

Instead, he was pissed.

She'd tried to steal this from him, and that was bullshit.

"Hello Olivia," he said before slowly entering the room with methodical steps.

Her expression started as confusion—he assumed as she tried to place him—then her eyes widened when the pieces fell together.

"Pete?" she gasped.

"Well, at least you remember my name."

Nick entered behind him, still humming from the excitement of being a part of his brother—although he didn't know that part yet—coming into the world.

"You two know each other?"

Maverick nodded slowly, keeping his gaze glued on the child suckling from his mother's breast. "We do. And I think Olivia has some things she needs to explain." Finally, he drew his eyes to his oldest son. "Would you mind giving us a minute?"

Nick's gaze volleyed between Olivia's now pale face and Mav's clenched jaw.

"Um, sure. I'll go down and grab something to eat in the cafeteria. Do you want anything?"

"Coffee would be great."

Without another word, Nick disappeared, and Maverick sat down on the edge of Olivia's bed.

"We can skip the part where I ask for a DNA test; we both know that's simply a formality. How about you explain why you thought it would be a good idea to keep my son from me, and then I'll explain what's going to happen next."

She was quiet for a beat, and at first Maverick thought she wasn't going to respond. At least she had the decency to not try and deny the paternity. Then she shifted the baby to her other breast—leaving the boob he'd just been feeding from exposed. The angry-red nipple was in stark contrast to her creamy white skin. A part of her anatomy he'd taken so much pleasure from the night they were together was now providing sustenance for their child. He found it erotic as fuck, and had to give himself an internal shake.

Do not let her distract me with her boobs. I'm fucking pissed.

"I didn't try to keep him from you," she said quietly. "I wanted to tell you."

"Oh, come on, Olivia. You knew exactly how to find me."

Her chin lifted defiantly. "I thought so, too. Turns out, it wasn't so easy. After I found out I was pregnant, I went back to Flannigan's to try and get your last name, or your phone number, or some way to get in contact with you. The men behind the bar all acted like they'd never heard of you and treated me like I was some crazy stalker."

Fuck. He remembered Derrick telling him how he'd saved him from one of his bad dates looking for him. He'd had no idea it'd been Olivia.

Her voice was soft but strong as she continued. "And even though I was humiliated, I still left my name and number and asked them to give it to you. I emphasized how important it was that I talk to you. When a month went by and I hadn't heard from you, I decided it was for the best."

That calmed his ire a little. He didn't like admitting he'd played a role in why she hadn't been able to get in touch with him. Had he told his brother why he'd been coming into the bar every week, this could have been avoided.

Still, that didn't excuse when he woke up the next day and found her gone.

"Well, darlin', if you hadn't snuck out of the hotel like a thief in the night, you'd have had my name and number. Imagine my surprise to find your side of the bed empty and cold the next morning when I reached for you. I thought we'd had a real connection that night."

"I know." Her whisper sounded contrite now. "I was ashamed of what I'd done."

He cocked his head. "Really? You didn't give me the impression of a woman ashamed of her sexuality." He couldn't help but smile as he thought back to that night. "Far from it, actually."

"I wasn't ashamed of sleeping with you. That part was incredible. But I'd lied to you, and I knew it was wrong."

His eyebrows knitted in confusion. "What did you lie about? Are you married?"

"No! Of course not! I didn't lie about that. Just, what I did for a living, and—"

He cut her off. "You're not an ER nurse?"

"No," she huffed out a laugh. "I'm an OB/GYN." Her voice dropped an octave, "So I knew there was a good chance I could get pregnant that night."

"But you were on birth control."

She shot him a look, and the truth dawned on him.

"So you *weren't* on birth control," he uttered. "And you *wanted* to get pregnant."

He could see her swallow hard before slowly nodding her head.

Inside, Maverick was pissed all over again as the pieces fell into place.

"And you thought I was the perfect sperm donor that you could walk away from without a second glance back."

Her silence spoke volumes.

"Well, I've got some bad news, darlin'. You aren't walking away from me. At least not with my son. Not without a helluva fight."

CHAPTER NINE

Olivia

Oh. Hell. No.

That was exactly what she'd been afraid of.

She lifted her son onto her shoulder to burp him, his bare skin warm against hers. She'd just vowed to protect this little guy, and that's what she was going to do.

Do not show fear.

She looked Pete in the eye. "What does that mean, exactly?"

"I have a few demands," he said as he began to unbutton his shirt.

"What are you doing?" she gasped.

He shot her an annoyed look. "Relax. I'm bonding with my son."

He held out his hands, gesturing that he wanted to hold the baby, and Olivia reluctantly handed him over. Pete moved to the chair by her bed and nestled the now-sleeping newborn against his hairy chest and gently patted his back.

The sight made her solar plexus feel tight.

"Have you chosen a name?" he asked as he stared down at the infant. It struck her how much the two resembled one another.

"Sawyer Evan."

"Hi Sawyer. I'm your dad."

He uttered the words so affectionately, she felt dizzy.

"So you have no objections to his name?"

"To Sawyer? No, not at all. As long as his last name is Mitchell, I'm agreeable."

Pete's last name is Mitchell.

She made a note of it, then sighed, not committing to anything.

"So, how do you see this working, Pete? Are we going to be able to come to a custody arrangement?"

He shook his head. "No need."

Relief swept through her body. He wasn't going to fight her over custody.

Then he dropped the hammer. "Since he's going to live with me." He glanced up at her. "You're invited too, of course."

"Um, excuse me?"

"I'm not missing out on raising my son this time, Olivia. I did that once and have lived with that regret—no way am I doing it again. We can do it together, or I can fight you for custody. But I have to tell you, I like my chances. I have deep pockets to hire the best attorneys in the state, twenty-five years of military service, a high eight-figure portfolio, and a flexible schedule to impress a judge with. What about you? How quickly are you planning on going back to work?"

It was a good thing she was lying down, because otherwise she might have fallen. He knew exactly how to wound her. Still, she wasn't going to let him bully her.

"I'm confident a judge wouldn't take a breastfeeding child from his mother, no matter how much money his father has in the bank."

"Okay, but again, once you go back to work, I don't think breastfeeding will matter. I can bottle feed him your breast milk while I'm at home with him, and you're at your job. I'll have to wait for, what—six weeks? Twelve? How much time were you planning on taking off?"

Her mouth opened and closed several times as she searched for the words to reply.

"Hey, Dad. Here's your cof—"

Nick stopped short in the doorway when he saw Pete's shirt open, and Sawyer snuggled against his chest under a receiving blanket.

He walked in slowly and looked back and forth between Olivia and his father. "What am I missing here?"

Pete carefully stood and transferred the baby back into Olivia's waiting arms. She hugged her son tight, never wanting to let him go again. Maybe she'd run away with him if she got the chance.

After he buttoned his shirt, he clasped Nick's shoulder. "Let's go for a walk." He paused before walking out the door, as if he'd read her mind. "I'll be back, Olivia. Don't get any crazy ideas. That won't help your situation."

"I just gave birth two hours ago," she snarked. "The only idea I have is to get some much-needed, and well-deserved rest."

That brought him back into the room with a softer expression. "I can put him in the bassinet for you so you can sleep."

"No," she said as she gently rubbed her cheek against the soft tufts of hair. "I want hold him a little while longer."

"I won't be long."

She wasn't sure if it was a promise or a warning.

CHAPTER TEN

Maverick

"What was that all about?" Nick asked the second they stepped into the hall. "You obviously know her. Intimately, by the looks of it."

Maverick took a swig from the coffee cup Nick had brought him from the cafeteria as he chose his next words carefully.

"You're right. We dated." He paused briefly. "Nine months ago." He didn't say anything more to let what he'd said sink in.

"So... her son... Sawyer..."

He stayed quiet, letting Nick process things.

"*Is my half-brother?*" His voice rose. "Are you telling me that I held your ex-girlfriend's hand while she gave birth to my sibling? What the fuck, Dad? Were you going to tell any of us?"

Maverick stopped in his tracks and formed a 'T' with his hands. "Time out. First of all, I understand you're upset, but watch your tone. I'm still your father. Secondly, she wasn't my girlfriend, per se. But I did like her a lot." He decided not to go into further detail about what had transpired between them. "And lastly, I had no idea she was pregnant until you sent that picture."

"That's why you came here right away."

"Yeah."

From the moment he'd seen her again, he was pulled to her. Just like he'd been the night they met, when she'd blown through the door at Flannigan's like a hurricane and turned his world upside down.

Then he held his infant son against his chest and thought about how much he'd missed out on with Nick and Nash. That wasn't happening this time. She might have thought she was getting a sperm donor that night, but she had another thing coming now. There was no way he was walking away. Not without a fight.

"Do you think she hired me because I'm your son?"

"I doubt she even knew." Again, he didn't want to air their dirty laundry—that they'd left the bar together an hour after meeting and got naked in a hotel room without even knowing each other's last names. "She seemed pretty surprised to see me."

"That's true. And she never asked anything about you whenever I talked to her. I think if she were trying to get to you, she'd have found a way to bring you up at least once."

"That's not her style. If she wanted to talk to me, she would have come to me directly, not played some silly game and made my twenty-one-year-old son an intermediary."

"Yeah, you're right." He chuckled. "Although I guess I still was the intermediary."

"I guess so."

They'd started walking again when Nick asked quietly, "So why didn't she come to you?"

"I think she tried, but wires got crossed and we didn't connect again. I think she took it as a sign that I wouldn't be supportive."

Nick snorted. "She doesn't know you very well, huh?"

"Not yet." But she was going to.

"So, what are you going to do, Dad?"

"I think..." He paused. What he was going to say was going to sound crazy, but he knew in his gut it was what he wanted. "I'm going to marry her."

Nick came to an abrupt halt and turned to him. "*What*? You can't be serious."

Maverick stopped, too. "Dead serious."

"She didn't even tell you she was pregnant, Dad. What makes you think she'd even say yes?"

Doing his best Marlon Brando impression, Maverick replied, "I'm going to make her an offer she can't refuse."

****

Olivia

"Don't wake her!" A hushed female voice pulled Olivia from her twilight sleep.

"I'm not going to! I just want to see my nephew!"

That voice she recognized as her twin's.

That meant the other voice had to be his girlfriend Hope.

"And that's going to wake her, dumbass!"

Olivia smiled without opening her eyes. She loved that Hope didn't take any of Evan's shit. He'd bulldoze anyone who let him, and she most-definitely did not let that happen.

"I'm awake," Olivia said as she slowly opened her eyes. Sawyer was still nestled against her chest.

"Oh, Liv," Evan gushed as put his finger in the baby's grip and softly shook it. "He's perfect."

"Do you want to hold him?"

"Yes!" Hope responded immediately as she stepped forward.

Evan body-blocked his girlfriend, then slowly turned his head to look at her over his shoulder. "*I'm* the uncle and godfather. I get to be the first person outside of his mom and hospital staff to hold him."

"Technically, we're hospital staff," Hope reminded him.

"Not in the maternity ward. Here we're just visitors."

Olivia chimed in. "I hate to burst your bubble, but Nick already beat you to it."

"Who's Nick?"

"The kid who drove me to the hospital and held my hand when my birth coach," she made a point of looking directly at Evan, "was snowed in—even though I told him not to go to the Cape—and didn't make it to the hospital in time. Oh, and, um, his dad also held him."

"His dad?"

How was she going to explain *that* to her brother?

Olivia realized she was too damn tired to worry about it. She'd tell him later.

"It's a long story, and I need to rest."

"Then give me my nephew and take a nap." Her brother gently pulled the sleeping baby from her and cradled him in his arms. As he stared down at Sawyer with a goofy grin, he added, "We only came to see him, anyway."

"Oh my god, Evan. You're such an asshole," Hope exclaimed.

"Language," Olivia reprimanded as she closed her eyes. She was a mom now. It was her job to make sure people didn't swear in front of her kid.

"You're already getting this mom thing down," a deep voice said from the other side of the bed, then she felt lips brush her forehead.

Why was someone kissing her forehead?

"Who are you?" her brother's voice demanded.

"Pete Mitchell. My friends call me Maverick. I'm Sawyer's dad."

She knew Evan was going to lose his shit over the bomb Pete just dropped, but she was too tired to care at the moment. She'd deal with it when she woke up. She was also going to have a chat with Pete about the art of timing.

She remembered the night at the bar when she'd gone back to try to find him, and how there'd been confusion if they were talking about the same person because they were calling him two different names. Now she understood why. Although she didn't understand how he got Maverick from Pete.

Then it hit her. He'd flown jets for the Navy. Maverick—Pete Mitchell—Top Gun.

"Maverick," she giggled with her eyes closed. "I get it now." Had she known his last name before today, it might have all made sense sooner.

"*Sawyer's* dad? Liv—what the hell is he talking about?" her brother groused.

"Language," she reminded again. "And, yes, he's Sawyer's dad. I'm too tired to explain, E. I just pushed an eight-pound human from my body, and I'm exhausted."

The covers were pulled up to her shoulders and another kiss to her forehead. She recognized the masculine smell—the same one from nine months ago, and for some reason it made her feel content.

"Go to sleep, darlin'," Pete's voice murmured in her ear. "I'll deal with your brother and stay with Sawyer until you wake up."

For the first time in a long time, she was able to completely relax. She didn't have to worry—someone else was going to handle things.

With that knowledge, she dozed off, knowing deep down she was in good hands.

CHAPTER ELEVEN

Olivia

Her eyes fluttered open; the light from the window was beginning to fade. What time was it? Where was she?

Suddenly, she was wide awake and sat up with a start.

Where was her baby?

How could she have slept so soundly? Did she sleep through his crying? She was already fucking up.

"He's right next to you, asleep in his bassinet," came a deep voice from the corner of the room.

Olivia saw Pete—Maverick—get out of a chair next to the window and walk toward her. She couldn't decide if she was relieved he was still there or scared.

"How long was I asleep?"

"Not even two hours. He's been out the whole time."

That made her feel a little better—about her mothering skills, anyway.

Maverick sat down on her bed next to her with a tentative smile.

His close proximity made her heart beat faster. "Whe—where are Evan and Hope?"

"They went to grab a bite to eat with your parents. A lovely couple, by the way."

"*You met my parents?*"

He chuckled. "Your brother made sure to introduce me."

Fucking Evan.

"I'll bet that was awkward."

"A little. But when I explained I intended on marrying you, they relaxed and tried to get to know me better."

She closed her eyes tight. "Uhhh, you did what?"

"Explained I intended on marrying you. Preferably before we leave the hospital, but I understand if you want to wait and plan for something in another month or two. I was thinking small and intimate, maybe even a destination wedding once you've been cleared to travel, and then a bigger party down the road. But I'm open to a big wedding and reception right away if that's what you've always had your heart set on."

She shook her head as if trying to fix where her brain was obviously short-circuiting.

"Are you insane? I'm not marrying you."

"Why not? You obviously liked me at one point—enough to get pregnant by me. On purpose."

"Liking someone is not a good enough reason to marry them."

With a shrug, he countered, "I'm the father of your child; that's a good reason."

"No, it's not. People all over the world have children every day without the benefit of marriage."

"So you admit it'd be a benefit."

"Stop trying to twist my words!"

"Okay, how about this." His tone got noticeably icier. "Marrying me is better than spending hundreds of thousands of dollars on a custody battle you won't win."

She glared at him. He had the upper hand and they both knew it. Still, she dug her heels in.

"I have a boyfriend."

"Really? Where is he? You'd think he'd be here for such an important event in your life."

"He's—he's snowed in. He went skiing in Vermont and is stuck there."

"Well, break it to him over text so he doesn't hurry back."

"I'm not marrying you," she reiterated. "And unless you want to be thrown out of this hospital room, you'll stop talking about it. I just pushed a tiny human out of my vagina not more than twelve hours ago. I don't have the energy for this argument."

She was going to milk that for as long as she could.

He studied her for a minute, as though he was trying to decide whether or not to call her bluff. He must have sensed she wasn't bluffing, because he didn't say anything more.

Just then Rose walked in with a clipboard and looked at Maverick. Olivia could tell she was curious about who he was, but all she said was, "I have to examine mama, so you need to step out into the hall."

"Yes, of course," he said, and immediately exited the room.

Rose put on a pair of blue gloves, then pulled the blankets off her and pulled up her gown while Olivia opened her legs. She knew the drill—she'd just never been on this end of it before.

"How are you feeling, my friend?" Rose asked as she probed and prodded Olivia's beat up female anatomy.

"As good as can be expected."

"You didn't tear, so that's good. Everything looks like it's recovering fine."

Rose helped Olivia get situated back under the blankets and picked up the clipboard from where she'd set it on the side table next to the bed.

"You've been able to nurse him without any problems?"

"He latched on with the second try."

Rose brought the clipboard down in front of her and looked at Olivia with an affectionate smile. "You did amazing, you know. Way better than I did when our roles were reversed."

"That's because I had you for my doctor. I was so relieved when you walked through the door."

Her friend laughed. "So was the poor kid whose hand you were squeezing."

"He was great, wasn't he?"

"Yeah, he was. I love how he proclaimed himself an honorary uncle once we put Sawyer in your arms."

"Yeah..." Olivia's voice trailed off. "There's a funny story behind that."

****

Maverick

The tiny powerhouse that had come in to examine Olivia walked out of her room and straight toward him. Based on the fast, no-nonsense click of her shoes as she approached, he assumed Olivia had told her who he was.

He was still mulling over whether or not she really had a boyfriend. His gut told him she was lying.

"Rose Baker," she said as she thrust out her hand. "I'm Olivia's doctor and business partner. I understand we need to get you a daddy ID bracelet."

That made him smile. "Yeah. I'd appreciate that."

They went to the nurse's station, and she went to work on the computer without saying anything, then disappeared, only to return a minute later with the ID bracelet.

"So, when her boyfriend gets here, does he get one, too?"

She squinted her eyes at him, like she was confused. "Only the parents get them."

That didn't answer his question.

"She's a great person and a phenomenal doctor," Rose said quietly as she attached the plastic to his wrist. "She's going to be a wonderful mother."

It felt like a warning rather than an observation, and he wondered what Olivia had told her.

He glanced down at the writing now attached to his wrist. Where it said baby, it read 'Sawyer Evan Mitchell,' with Pete's name listed as father.

Seeing it in writing seemed to make it more real.

"Well, then little Sawyer is in luck, because I'm a pretty great dad, and lucky for him, I have experience. So he'll have two devoted parents."

CHAPTER TWELVE

Maverick

Olivia's family returned from dinner, and he decided to take the opportunity to go home, pack an overnight bag, and make sure his house was ready to bring a baby into it.

Fuck, he didn't have any baby furniture.

He called Gabe, the oldest of his younger brothers. He had kids, so he was the obvious choice for help.

"What's up, Mav?" he answered in a chipper tone.

"I don't exactly know how to say this, so I'm just going to come out and say it. I just learned I have a newborn son, and when I say newborn, I mean he was born earlier today."

"Are you shitting me?"

"I am not. It's a long story, and I promise I will tell you about it soon. Right now, though, I need your help. I need some basic furniture for when he comes home tomorrow. Like, at least a bassinet and changing table. Can you help me out?"

"I can do that, but I am going to expect full details."

Maverick smiled into the receiver. He could always count on his brothers when he needed them.

"I know, and I will tell you everything, I promise. Just not now. I have to get back to the hospital."

He wanted to be there in case this alleged boyfriend of hers was real and showed up.

"Let me ask you this—is this hush-hush or can I enlist the other brothers for help?"

"Nick knows, for the record, but I don't care who helps; it's not like this is something I'm going to hide. I just need it done before tomorrow, probably late morning—early afternoon-ish."

"What's my budget?"

"There is none. Just get the best quality. I don't care what it costs."

"If you would have given me notice, I could've built something."

"Well, considering I just found out today, that would have been hard to do."

"*You just found out today?* Man, I can't wait to hear this story. What about his mom?"

"She's coming here, too."

At least he hoped she was.

"Damn, Mav. Are you nuts? You just earned your freedom, man! Now you're starting over with diapers and bottles and sleepless nights."

"It's not like I planned this," he grumbled. "But, at least I know what to expect, right?"

"I guess." Gabe didn't sound convinced.

"It's not exactly like I have a choice here. I have a son. What would you suggest I do?"

His brother was as honorable as Maverick. He had to understand there was no other option.

"I don't know, dude. Next time, wrap your cock better? Pull out? Get snipped?"

"Thanks for the stellar advice, asshole. I'll take it into consideration *next time*. But right now, I'm bringing a baby home tomorrow." At least that was the plan. "Can you help me or not?"

"Just bustin' your balls, bro. That's not something I get to do every day, so I'm going to take advantage of it while I have the chance."

"Go ahead, yuck it up now 'cuz when I get home tomorrow, that shit will be on lockdown, you understand? It will be nothing but fucking rainbows and unicorns around Olivia and Sawyer."

"Aw, I like his name."

"Yeah, me too."

"Did you pick it out?"

"No, that was all his mom. I just provided the last name."

"So she's letting him have your last name? She's not hyphenating or anything? I hear that's becoming more common these days, especially if the parents aren't married."

"Yeah, well, I'm hoping to take care of that, too." He didn't give a shit about this supposed boyfriend.

"Shut. The. Fuck. Up. You are not going to marry this girl?"

"Uh, why the hell not? She's brilliant, funny, beautiful, and the mother of my son. I'd be a fool not to."

The more he thought about it, the more he was convinced he was right.

"Dude...." Maverick could picture his brother shaking his head on the other end. "At least make sure you get a prenup."

"Yeah, of course."

A prenup. He hadn't even considered that. He would have married her in the hospital chapel without one today. Maybe it was a good thing she'd slowed his roll.

"Alright, if I'm going on a quest for baby furniture, I probably need to get started before the stores close."

"Thanks, Gabe. I owe you."

"No, you don't. That's what brothers do. Besides, I'm pretty sure you've saved my ass more than once; it's the least I can do."

"Well, I appreciate it."

"Send me some pictures of my nephew and his mom. She's hot, isn't she?"

She's gorgeous. And probably closer to his brother's age.

"You don't need to worry about what she looks like," he snarled. "But I will send you some pictures of the baby when I get back to the hospital."

Gabe didn't even try to disguise his delight at getting a rise out of him. "Later, big daddy," he said, then clicked off.

He couldn't help but grin, even as he muttered, "Asshole," before tossing his phone in his bag.

Chapter Thirteen

Olivia

Her parents kissed her cheek, then promised to be by the next day to help her take Sawyer home and get him situated.

"That's okay," Olivia said with a weak smile. "I'm not sure when I'm going to be released. I don't want you guys to have to wait around all day."

"Yes, it will be such a hardship, taking turns holding our grandson while we wait," her father deadpanned.

"I just don't..." she trailed off when she noticed her brother with furrowed brows, scrutinizing her from the chair by the window. Hope had gotten called to the hospital prosthetic lab that she oversaw and left him there to silently judge her.

Olivia pulled her shoulders back and forced a bright smile as she looked at her parents in the doorway. "Don't get here too early."

"We won't, pumpkin." Her mom's eyes shone. "Congratulations, he's beautiful. See you tomorrow."

The silence was deafening once their parents left. Finally Evan growled, "You wanna tell me what the fuck is going on?"

"Language," she sighed.

Her brother was undeterred. "Spill it, Liv. You forbade me from talking about your baby daddy—said he didn't want anything to do with the baby. Then you tell me over the Fourth that you got pregnant with a one-night stand whose last name you didn't know. And now this guy shows up right after you've given birth, saying he's the father and talking to mom and dad about marrying you?"

She bit her bottom lip. Evan wouldn't believe her if she tried explaining it.

He shook his head. "Seems a little too convenient, if you ask me."

"He really is Sawyer's dad, E."

"So he just gets to show up now that the baby's here and act like everything's great? Where the hell was he when you were puking your guts out, or having Popeyes cravings in the middle of the night?" She knew she should have never shared that story with her twin. "Or needed furniture assembled?"

"I know what it looks li—"

"Trust me," came Maverick's voice from the door. "I wish I would have been there for all that." He walked to where Sawyer slept in the bassinet next to her bed and stared at the sleeping boy for a second before looking at Olivia. "Unfortunately, that wasn't the case. The only thing we can do now is move forward and raise our son together."

Together. His idea of what that looked like seemed to be vastly different than hers.

"We don't even know anything about you," Evan grumbled.

"What do you want to know? I'm the oldest of four boys. Grew up in Boston, earned my degree in aeronautical engineering at MIT. As soon as I graduated, I joined the Navy and flew jets for twenty-three of my twenty-five years with them. My parents are still alive and living in Florida. I have two sons with my ex-wife, who I'm on good terms with. My youngest boy joined the Navy last year straight out of high school, and my oldest goes to Boston U and helped deliver Sawyer today."

"Yeah, how did *that* happen?"

He shrugged. "I'm going with kismet."

Evan eyed him suspiciously. "Do you work now? Or are you going to rely on Olivia to pad your Navy pension?"

Maverick chuckled quietly, but didn't seem rattled at the intrusive line of questioning. "I'm the silent partner in several businesses and my investment portfolio meets my needs and then some just fine."

"Define fine," her brother challenged.

Finally, it seemed like Maverick's tolerance meter for Evan was pegged.

With a firm tone and raised brow, he replied, "Olivia and Sawyer will never want for anything, and if Olivia chooses to work, it will be because she *wants* to, not because she *needs* to."

The two men stared at each other in some type of testosterone-filled standoff.

Little Sawyer's cries broke the tension, and Maverick reached down to pick him up, then handed him to Olivia when she murmured, "He must be hungry."

Evan took that as his cue to leave, so he stood, but not without commenting, "I'll be back tomorrow with Mom and Dad to help take you home." Although his remark was directed at her, she knew it was meant to be a warning to Maverick.

He responded in kind. "I look forward to seeing you tomorrow. But you needn't worry about helping them home, since they'll be coming to my place."

The standoff began again.

Olivia decided to let the two men have their pissing contest and not interject that she was, in fact, going back to her house and not Maverick's.

Finally, Evan broke his stare and glanced at Olivia, who was now feeding Sawyer.

"I'll see you tomorrow."

"Love you, E. Thanks for coming today."

"Wild horses couldn't have kept me away." He glared at Maverick, then his face softened when he looked back at Olivia. "Love you, too, Sis."

She wasn't expecting Maverick's soft laugh, followed by, "I like him," once her brother left the room.

"Could have fooled me."

"He obviously loves you and is just looking out for you and Sawyer, so how can I not?"

"You realize we're not going to your house tomorrow, right?"

He was quiet for a minute while he watched her and the baby, as if calculating how he wanted to proceed.

Finally, he murmured, "You don't want to fight me on this, Olivia. You won't win. At least not in the long run."

That made her feel helpless—something she despised, and she sassed, "So, you expect me to just uproot my life and move in with you? Isn't that convenient—for you."

"Look, I know it's not ideal, but since I just found out this morning that I'm a father again, while you've had, I'm guessing, at least seven months to get used to the idea, it will have to do for now."

"This isn't fair," she whispered as she stared down at her nursing son.

"But you think lying to me about being on birth control and getting pregnant on purpose was?"

"I didn't think I'd ever see you again."

He scoffed. "So that's supposed to make it better? I'd have had a son out in the world that I knew nothing about, Olivia."

"Yeah, exactly—key words: knew nothing about."

She realized from his clenched jaw that probably wasn't the approach she should have taken.

"Did you ever stop to think he might have done a genealogy test in the future? How do you think that would have turned out when he showed up on my doorstep and announced he's my son? Did you think he wouldn't be bitter that you let him grow up without a father, or I wouldn't be angry that you kept my child from me?"

She swallowed hard.

Well, when he says it like that...

"I told you, I tried to find you."

"You should have tried harder."

"What would you have had me do, Pete? Should I have hired a private investigator to chase you down? For all I knew, you'd lied to me about co-owning the bar. Heck, I wasn't even sure if Pete was your real name, since the other owner of the bar seemed to have no idea who I was talking about."

He sat down at the foot of her bed, his expression softer.

"How about this—you agree to stay with me while we figure things out. That way we can get to know each other, and I'll be able to help take care of Sawyer so you can rest and take it easy."

Having help did sound appealing. She knew that was the advice she gave new mothers—take whatever help was offered. She usually added the caveat, unless it was going to cause more work down the road.

She narrowed her eyes at him. "I have two cats."

"I have a big house and am not allergic."

"Will I have my own room?"

He shrugged and casually replied, "Sure," like it didn't matter to him one way or another.

She still hesitated, so he added, "I think we should get to know each other better, don't you? And we both need to bond with our son. Living under the same roof solves that."

She picked some lint from her blanket and nodded. "You're right, we do need to get to know each other, since it seems we're going to be in each other's lives for at least the next eighteen years, whether we like the idea or not."

He looked her in the eye, his mouth twitching like he was fighting a grin. "On the contrary, I very much like the idea."

****

Maverick

"Why *your* house?" she demanded.

"It doesn't have to be my house, but I'm willing to bet mine is bigger."

She rolled her eyes. "I'm not exactly poor, you know."

"No, I'm sure you're quite comfortable. But I purposefully bought my place to accommodate two rambunctious adolescent boys at the time."

"How many bedrooms do you have?"

"Six. Plus eight bathrooms."

"Six? Why do you need six bedrooms?"

"I don't. But I liked the property and the neighborhood, so having a few extra guestrooms wasn't a dealbreaker." He flashed her a cocky smile. "It seems like it worked out for the best."

She put Sawyer over her shoulder to burp him, not taking her eyes off Maverick. At least she'd stopped arguing about moving in.

"You won't be mistreated. Scout's honor."

"So, can I have my boyfriend over?"

He felt the blood rush from his head, but fought not to react, since he knew that's what she wanted.

"No."

She raised her eyebrow at his cold, one-word response, but didn't argue. She better not have a fucking boyfriend.

"What about you? You're not going to have your girlfriend over?

"What makes you think I have a girlfriend?"

"Of course you do."

That made the corner of his mouth turn up. "Why do you say that?"

"I mean," she gestured toward him with her free hand. "Look at you. I'm sure women are lining up to—"

"Take me to a hotel and trick me into impregnating them?"

She laid Sawyer on the bed to change his diaper.

"Okay, if you're going to bring that up with every conversation we have, then I don't see the point of us talking anymore." She pointed to a bag on the floor. "Hand me those wipes and a diaper."

"Again," he said as he complied with her request and handed her the items. "You've had time to come to terms with being a mom. I'm still wrapping my head around having another child. When I woke up this morning my youngest had just turned nineteen, and then I found out I have a newborn. It's a lot to take in. I think I'm entitled to get a few more digs in while I process things."

"It doesn't make me want to stay with you."

"Move in," he corrected, then stood and picked up his freshly changed son. "You're moving in."

He stared down at the content baby in his arms. When the little guy smiled just as he started to doze off, Maverick thought his heart was going to burst from his chest.

"Let me amend that. You're moving in and marrying me."

He wasn't missing out on this again.

CHAPTER FOURTEEN

Olivia

Her hospital room had turned into Grand Central Station by nine the next morning. In addition to Maverick, her parents, Evan and Hope, and Steven had all dropped in, plus the hospital staff that stopped by to wish her well and, she suspected, to get a look at her baby daddy. She was sure word had gotten out. After all the visitors, she was more tired than she had been the day before.

Rose came in to check on her and took one look at her before barking, "Everyone has to leave. Right. Now. I need to examine Mama, then she needs to rest."

Maverick stood, slow to shuffle out with the grumbling crowd, and Olivia said softly, "He can stay."

Rose cocked her head. "You sure?"

She nodded. "I sleep better knowing he's there for Sawyer."

"Dad—you may come back in when I'm done with my examination," Rose announced loudly.

He turned around with a smile. "Is she going to be ready to go home soon?"

Rose eyed him as she put on her gloves. "If everything checks out, I'll get her discharge papers started."

Maverick nodded and closed the door.

"I hear he stayed all night with you."

Olivia stared at the ceiling as her vagina was on display for what seemed like the hundredth time in the span of a day.

"He did." She felt like she needed to justify it. "He was a great help with Sawyer so I didn't have to get out of bed to get him when it was time to nurse."

"Is he going to stay at the house with you? At least until you're able to walk easier?"

"Um. He wants me to move in with him."

Her friend raised her eyebrows as she peeled off her gloves. "Oh? Is that what you want?"

"I wouldn't mind the help," Olivia admitted. "And he's right—we both need to bond with the baby and get to know each other better."

"So, it'd only be temporary."

Olivia hesitated, not sure how to answer that, so Rose asked, "It wouldn't be temporary?"

"I don't know. At this point, I'm just taking it one day at a time."

Rose squeezed her hand. "That's all you need to do right now. I don't have to tell you that in addition to being sore, your hormones are going to be all over the place. I think letting him take care of you is a great idea."

"You do?"

"He seems like a good guy. I made Chad do a quick background search on him last night—everything appears to be on the up and up. Not even a traffic ticket. He owns a number of businesses and is involved with a few charities. There's nothing on his social media that suggests he's been seriously involved with anyone and based on all the pictures with him and his kids, he seems like a good dad. Plus, his house looks freaking amazing."

That made her feel better. Still, she asked, "How do you know?"

"Google Maps."

"Jesus, you sure you're not in the CIA?"

Her friend shook her head. "I don't have time for the CIA."

"Well, thanks, but you didn't have to go to all that trouble."

"Gotta look out for my girl."

"I appreciate it. Tell Chad thanks, too."

"Oh, I already thanked him last night," she replied with a wink. "He demanded payment in full for helping me."

"And I'm sure you were happy to oblige."

"Yes. I. Was."

"You better watch it, or you're going to find yourself pregnant again."

"Nope. He took care of that a few months ago; we decided four was plenty."

"I don't know how you do it—four kids, a husband, and a successful career. You're freaking wonder woman. I'm on the verge of an anxiety attack every time I think about trying to raise one kid and keep my job."

"You better plan on keeping your job. I can't do this alone."

"Unless I win the lottery, you have nothing to worry about. Combining a career and motherhood will just take some getting used to. I'll figure it out."

Rose smiled at her. "I have no doubt you will. Having a great partner makes all the difference. You'll see. Although, I'm curious about something he said. Are you seeing someone else?"

****

Maverick

"A fucking Rolls Royce? Are you kidding me?" Olivia groused after he got out of his Cullinan as she waited at the curb in her wheelchair holding Sawyer.

He was unapologetic as he took the baby from her while the nurse helped her to the car.

"I wanted an SUV, and I wanted the best. Problem solved."

She pursed her lips, but didn't say anything else as she got situated in the passenger seat while he strapped the newborn into the new car seat in the back.

He paused to stare at the perfect little boy he'd helped create, asleep without a care in the world. He was a dad again—how amazing was that? While the concept hadn't even been in the realm of possibility when Maverick woke up yesterday, he was ready to turn his world upside down for this baby—and his mother.

Oliva was quiet the entire drive, until murmuring, "Wow, that's a lot of cars," when they pulled into his drive.

All three of his brothers' cars, along with Nick's truck, were in the loop out front.

"Those aren't mine. Mine are in the garage. You're about to be bombarded with Mitchell men. Sorry."

Her smile was tired but bright. "Don't be. I want to meet your family."

He liked the idea of introducing her to them.

Rubbing a spot on his chest that suddenly seemed to ache, he asked, "You do?"

"Sure. They're Sawyer's family, too. It's important that I know who's going to be around him."

Of course. It had nothing to do with her wanting to know about him.

"Right. Well, they're boisterous, but every one of them would give you the shirt off his back."

"Or drive you to the hospital when you're in labor and hold your hand while you gave birth," she mused.

"That, too."

He clicked the garage door opener and waited for the door to go up.

"So, how did your boyfriend take the news?"

"What news?"

"That you're moving in with me."

"Oh, um, he—he's not happy, obviously. But he said he'll wait for me."

Maverick snorted. "He's going to be waiting a long time."

They pulled into one of the empty stalls, and he was more convinced than ever that she was lying. If he were her boyfriend, it'd take an army to stop him from thwarting her moving in with another man. He also wouldn't have gone skiing so close to her due date.

Hell, if this guy was real, Maverick had done her a favor.

Shutting off the vehicle, he took a deep breath. *This is it.* He hoped she liked his place. He'd had it professionally redecorated once the boys hit their late teens and he could have nice things again. Still, he knew the décor was more on the masculine side.

"You have carte blanche on almost anything you want to redecorate or change."

"*Almost* anything?"

Maverick grinned, "I'll have to overrule you if you want to make changes to my car garage."

She gestured to the shiny black Ford F150 and the slate grey Porsche 911 he'd pulled between.

"You have more cars than this?"

He noticed her surveying the four-stall garage. Everything was neat and orderly, just how he liked it.

"A few."

"Well, if the outside and *this* garage are any indication, I'm sure the inside is lovely."

"There's a difference between lovely and homey. I want you to feel at home."

"Pete—"

He didn't like how she said his name and opened the driver's door without letting her finish her thought.

"Let me show you inside."

She slipped out the passenger side and had opened the back door before he was able to come around.

"When did you have time to get a car seat, by the way?"

"I ordered it online and had it delivered to the hospital while you were sleeping this morning."

"Aren't you efficient."

"When I need to be." He let his eyes run over her body. "But I also know how to take my time when I want to."

Her cheeks turned an adorable shade of pink, and she ducked inside to unclick the car seat.

He politely moved her out of the way with, "Let me get him."

"I can do it."

She fumbled around, cursing under her breath, then finally poked her head outside. "You can go ahead."

He bit back a smile, but didn't say anything as he reached inside.

"The stroller for this is in the back," he called from inside the cab. "You're supposed to be able to use it with the car and the stroller so you never have to take him out between the two."

"I looked at those, but they were a little more than I wanted to spend."

"That's not going to be an issue anymore. If you want it, you get it. I can afford it."

"You realize I make a nice salary, right?"

"Of course. But my salary affords me the luxury of not looking at price tags."

"How do you have so much money? Are you a trust fund kid? You were in the Navy for twenty-five years."

That made him chuckle as he pulled the seat out. "Not a trust fund kid. My dad was a mechanic and my mom an elementary school secretary. I went to college on scholarship. I backed a few startups that ended up paying big, which I then invested wisely."

"Impressive. I'll have to have you look at my 401k," she quipped.

"I know you're joking, but I would be happy to if you ever really want me to."

"Thanks."

They stood at the door leading to the house.

"Ready?" he asked with his hand on the knob.

She took a deep breath in and let it out slowly. "Yep."

****

Olivia

"Hello?" Maverick's deep voice bellowed as they walked through the laundry room. She noticed the litter box and knew Oscar and Honey were around there somewhere.

The laundry room led to a gourmet kitchen that looked like it belonged in a magazine. She glanced around the beautiful space.

Maybe I'll start cooking more.

The idea was terrific in theory, but she knew the odds of it actually happening were slim, at best. She wouldn't take that bet.

The house was quiet, so they walked further inside, and he called out again.

Nick poked his head over the railing. "We're up here, Dad!"

Maverick looked at her and hesitated at the foot of the wide staircase. "Can you handle the stairs?"

She appreciated his concern for her. "If I go slow, I should be fine."

"You sure? Because I can carry you."

That made her smile. "Trust me, I'm a doctor."

"Not an ER nurse," he teased as he took her hand and patiently helped her up the first step.

"Har har. You're never going to let that go, are you?"

"No, I will." Then he smirked. "Eventually."

Maverick held her hand while managing to keep the car seat holding Sawyer steady as Honey made an appearance, walking through their legs and trying to trip them down the stairs.

"Hi Honey. I'll scratch your ears when I'm sitting down, I promise."

"I thought you said you had two cats?"

"You probably won't see Oscar for a month. He doesn't like strangers." Which was why Rose had to meet Nick at her house to put him in the carrier. No way would Nick have been able to do that alone.

They got to the top of the stairs, and he directed her down the hall. They paused in front of the first room. "This can be your room—if you want."

Other than that it was larger than any she'd ever seen, it was a typical guestroom. The white furniture was sleek, and the décor was greys and blues—much like the rest of his house. The cat tree was set up in there.

"It's nice."

"Kind of boring," he supplied.

Olivia didn't say anything, and they kept walking toward male voices.

She gasped when she stepped through the threshold of the next room. It smelled like paint and there were drop cloths still on the floor, but inside was a nursery with a fresh coat of blue paint and larger than life jungle animals on the wall. There was also a crib with matching changing table and dresser. In the corner was a rug and bookshelf with a few board books and a rocking chair.

"This looks amazing, guys. Thanks," Maverick said to the four men who seemed to be anxiously watching her expression.

Meanwhile, she tried to find the words as she fought becoming a blubbering mess. These men had come together to put together a room for her son. Sawyer was now part of their family.

"The jungle theme is just giant stickers, so you can easily change it out if you don't like it," a guy who looked like a younger version of Maverick said.

"No," she finally managed. "It's perfect. Did you do all this today?"

"We got started last night," Nick said proudly.

"I can't believe you guys did this," she whispered as she looked around the room again, then back at the group. "Thank you."

"I know it still smells like paint," a handsome man with light brown hair said as he stepped forward. "But we figured it would be okay since his bassinet is set up in the master bedroom."

She wondered how hard it would be to move into her guestroom.

Maverick's hand came to the small of her back.

"Let me introduce you to everyone. That's Gabe," he pointed to the guy who looked most like him. "He's the second oldest. And that's Beau." The guy who'd told her about the bassinet waved. "And, you know Nick."

At that, Nick pulled her against his side to hug her around the shoulders. "Hey, Liv."

"Hi," she said with an affectionate smile.

Nick released her and Maverick returned his hand to her back as he continued. "And the baby of the family, Derrick, who you've met."

Her smile fell when she recognized the man from the bar. The one who'd said he had no idea who she was talking about.

His hair was the lightest of the men, but seeing them all together, she could see the family resemblance. She hadn't noticed it when she'd talked to him at Flannigan's.

He must have noticed her frown because he gave her a sheepish smile. "I'm sorry about that night; I thought you were someone else looking for my brother."

She wasn't going to cut him any slack.

"Nope. Just a woman pregnant with his child trying to get in touch with him so she could tell him."

Derrick closed his eyes and groaned. "I had no idea. You didn't look pregnant!"

Maverick half-coughed, half-laughed, obviously uncomfortable. He reached down to lift the car seat up. "And this little guy is Sawyer."

When the Mitchell men looked at the sleeping boy, they broke into matching grins, Nick included. Olivia hoped Sawyer inherited their smile.

"You're right, Nick. He does look like you," Gabe said as he stared at Sawyer.

Nick shrugged. "Well, that's what my mom said, anyway."

Maverick jerked his head up with a frown. "Your mom knows?"

"I hope it's okay that I told her."

He scrubbed his hand across his chin. "Yeah, of course. I'm sure she had plenty to say about it."

"Well, at first, she giggled and said, 'Better him than me,' but then she said she was happy for you."

"Sounds like Patricia," Beau said with a laugh.

It struck Olivia how much history these people had together, and that she was the outsider in this equation. Probably how Maverick felt at the hospital when she was surrounded by her family, friends, and colleagues.

"No, I think she really is," Nick said, defending his mom. "She wants him to be happy. I think she feels guilty that she and Ken are so happy while Dad has been alone."

"She doesn't need to worry about me," Maverick groused.

Derrick knelt down and stroked Sawyer's tight fist, making the baby whimper and shift in his seat. The man looked up at Olivia with a crooked grin. "He's definitely not alone now."

CHAPTER FIFTEEN

Olivia

She was stretched out on a chaise lounge, nursing Sawyer in front of the fire Maverick had built in the fireplace of the owner's suite before he walked his family out.

"Hey," he said quietly when he came in and tucked the throw around her. "I'm going to make dinner. Lasagna okay?"

Olivia cocked her head. "You're making lasagna?"

"Well, I'm going to put it in the oven. My housekeeper preps and freezes meals for me, so even though I don't cook I still have home-cooked meals regularly."

"That's brilliant."

He gave her a tender smile. "She'll be happy to have someone new to cook for. I think she's tired of making the same five things I ask for."

She moved Sawyer to her other breast, then sighed. "Pete, you know I can't move in here."

Tearing his gaze away from her exposed breast, she noticed him clench and unclench his jaw. "Actually, I don't see how you can't." His eyes locked with hers. "I will fight you for custody, Olivia. Your boyfriend's not worth it."

Her boyfr—? Oh yeah, she'd told him she had a boyfriend.

"You don't know that. This doesn't have to be a fight; I'm not a jerk, Pete. I'm willing to share custody."

"I'm not. And I'm not willing to let another man raise my son this time."

She glared at him. How could he be so insufferable? He'd seemed like such a good guy the night they'd met.

"Why? You said your boys' stepdad is a nice man."

"He is. It doesn't mean I'm willing to do it again."

"You don't honestly believe you'll win? There's no way a judge would keep a baby from his mother."

"I'm not suggesting you'll never get to see him. But it will be on my terms."

Olivia turned her gaze to her son suckling on her breast. She wasn't going to lose him; she didn't care what it cost. She'd go broke before she let that happen.

The irony of why she'd decided to have a one-night stand instead of going to a fertility clinic—so she wouldn't blow through her savings—wasn't lost on her.

His tone was gentler when he said, "Get to know me, Olivia. You'll find I'm not a bad guy."

"I never thought you were—until you started talking about taking my child from me."

"I don't want to take him from you, but I'm not going to miss out on raising him, either. Being married and living together solves everything."

"Everything except the fact we're not in love." She hastily added, "And I'm in love with someone else."

He shrugged. "Are ya, though? I mean, if you were my girlfriend, I would have hired a snowplow to get me to the hospital, but that's just me. And hey, we like each other—at least, I like you. And we certainly have sexual chemistry."

"*Had* sexual chemistry. Past tense."

He studied her face. "If you wanna believe that, sure. *Had.* Anyway, you have your own room."

"I have my own house."

"You're not a prisoner, darlin'. You can go anytime."

"I'm not going anywhere without my son."

"Well then, I guess you should probably get comfortable here."

****

Maverick

He brought a tray with two plates of lasagna, a basket of garlic bread, napkins, silverware, and water, and set it on the table in the sitting area next to the fireplace.

"Here, let me take him so you can eat," he said as he reached for Sawyer.

She protested. "He needs to be changed."

The corner of his mouth turned up. "I know how to change a diaper, darlin'."

Putting a towel down on his bed, along with wipes and a fresh diaper, Maverick laid the baby down and unsnapped his onesie to unfasten the dirty diaper while Sawyer kicked and wiggled.

"Little man," Maverick pleaded as he tried to clean his son's bottom. "Ya gotta hold still."

He looked over to see Olivia shaking with laughter as she took a bite of food.

With renewed determination, he lifted Sawyer's legs and slid the clean diaper under him, managing to get one tab fastened before the infant kicked again and sent the diaper askew.

"Son, work with me, here."

Olivia was at his side and took over—putting the diaper in place with one attempt.

"I think I'm liking my chances with a judge," she said smugly before picking the baby up and walking back to the chaise lounge. She laid him next to her and patted his tummy with one hand while continuing to eat with the other. It was impressive how effortless it was for her.

"I'm just out of practice," he said defensively as he cleaned up the bed and his hands before following her to the sitting area and picking up his plate. "It's like riding a bike; I'll get the hang of it again."

"If you say so."

Maverick stabbed his pasta with more gusto than necessary. He was embarrassed that he'd messed that up—and in front of her. She'd made it look so easy at the hospital.

While Patricia had been the primary caregiver for Nick and Nash, he'd helped. Not like he should have, but it wasn't because he was sitting on the couch drinking beer—he'd been deployed when each of the boys had come into the world.

Still, he'd changed diapers when he'd made it home, and tried to pitch in as much as Patricia would allow. She had her way of doing things and didn't like him messing up her routine, so he tried to respect that.

Perhaps he'd used it as an excuse not to be as present as he should have been.

Not this time.

"Maybe you can teach me."

That seemed to surprise her because she paused mid-bite, then set her fork down with her food still on it.

"Yeah. I can do that."

CHAPTER SIXTEEN

Olivia

Maverick took the dishes downstairs and handed her the remote to the TV. She clicked the power on and waited. Up popped a Bruins game, and she smiled.

Would she have even met Pete if the bar hadn't been full of hockey fans that night, and she'd had other seating choices? Maybe he wouldn't have been there if the game hadn't been on.

That night was the biggest butterfly effect moment of her life so far—hands down.

He returned twenty minutes later and immediately picked up a sleeping Sawyer and kissed his cheek as he carried him to the bassinet next to his bed.

"Do you think you can move that to my room?"

"Not without waking him up."

She weighed what having the cradle in here meant. "It's okay if he wakes up. It's more important that he sleeps in my room. It'll be easier for me to nurse him in the middle of the night if he's with me."

"What'll be easier is if you sleep in here with me, so I can help you when he wakes up."

She opened her mouth to object, but he cut her off. "I'm not going to try anything, Olivia. As sexy as I think you are, I recognize you're in no position to have sex. My bed has plenty of room for the both of us. It'll be fine."

"Sexy, yeah, sure."

He laid Sawyer down and stood up straight, pinning her with his stare.

"You have no idea how beautiful you are when you're caring for our son."

Oh, she had an idea. Watching this six-foot-three man be so delicate with their baby had been doing something to her, too.

She looked away, knowing she was blushing.

"I'll even wear pajamas," he said with a smirk.

Olivia couldn't help rolling her eyes. "How gallant of you."

Maverick seemed unfazed by her sarcasm. "I'm nothing if not thoughtful, darlin'."

Half an hour later she found herself gingerly stepping into his shower. It had more handles, buttons, faucets and nozzles than she knew what to do with.

"Oh!" she exclaimed out loud after she'd pushed a button and jets hit her from all directions. That was quickly followed by an, "Ohhh," as the warm water washed over her.

She'd only planned on a quick shower, but she ended up letting herself enjoy the experience.

"I just had a baby," she reasoned. "I've earned a long, luxurious shower."

As she toweled off with the fluffiest towel she'd ever used, she looked at her clothes lying on the floor and realized she didn't have anything clean to wear. Everything from the hospital had been dirty and stuffed into her bag.

She came out with her hair wrapped in a towel, wearing a navy-blue velour robe she'd found on a hook. Maverick sat bare-chested against the headboard with reading glasses on the end of his nose as he held a tablet in his hand.

He looked sexy as sin.

Swallowing hard, she said, "Mav?" to get his attention.

He looked up and froze for a second as he took her in. She knew she looked ridiculous swimming in his bathrobe. She hadn't worn makeup since the day before she went to the hospital.

Finally, a tender smile settled on his lips. "I like when you call me Mav."

She ignored his flirty remark. "I don't have any clean pajamas."

Setting the tablet aside, he pulled his glasses off before swinging his legs off the bed and walking to his dresser, where he opened the top drawer. He had on a pair of maroon and blue plaid pajama pants that did nothing to hide his sexy Adonis belt, and she couldn't avert her eyes if she wanted to.

"I've got a pair of boxers and a t-shirt you can sleep in." He held up the mentioned items, but she hesitated to take them.

"I... I don't have a clean bra, either. Or any clean clothes for that matter."

He tilted his head. "Do you usually sleep in a bra?"

"I just, uh." She paused then blurted out, "I'm probably going to leak milk in the middle of the night."

He handed the clothes to her. "That's what washing machines are for, sweetheart. And we can go get your things tomorrow, or better yet, get you a new wardrobe."

She pursed her lips. "That seems a bit extreme."

He shrugged. "I don't know how much your body has changed. Maybe you need new clothes."

"I have some things that should fit."

"Great. We can go tomorrow, or if you'd rather, we can hire movers to bring your things here."

"I don't need to hire movers."

What was she doing? It sounded like she was *agreeing* to go get her things tomorrow.

Putting her hands on her velour-belted hip, she added, "I don't need to move—period. I have a beautiful home that I love. A nursery with brand new furniture that doesn't smell like paint. And a nice young man that comes and plows my driveway..."

She threw the last part in to try and soften her demand.

He watched her with an amused expression and opened his mouth to say something when Sawyer let out a cry.

He gestured to the bed with his head. "Why don't you get comfy. I'll get him."

She stacked his lush pillows against the headboard and sank onto his comfortable memory-foam mattress. It was in stark contrast to the uncomfortable hospital bed she'd been lying on for the last two days.

Maverick gently placed the now-wailing baby in her arms. She had to admit, it was nice to just have him handed to her instead of having to bend over and pick him up. Not that she couldn't do it if she needed to.

I'm a strong, independent woman—I don't need help; I can handle this.

But damn, it was nice not having to all the time.

****

Maverick

He set his alarm to go off every three hours. Since little Sawyer was more than happy to sleep, they had to wake him so Olivia could nurse. Fortunately, after eating and getting changed, he immediately fell back to sleep, content and happy.

When his alarm went off at three a.m., she looked over at him, her hair mussed and circles under her eyes.

"You don't have to get up, too. There's no point in both of us being sleep deprived."

"I'm here to help you, darlin'. Of course I'm going to get up with you."

He did, however, doze off once he'd put the baby in her arms. Feeling the mattress shift woke him, and he slowly sat up.

"I've got him," he protested when he saw her walking toward the bassinet.

"It's fine—I need to use the bathroom, anyway. Go back to sleep."

Maverick didn't completely relax until he felt the bed dip with her weight next to him.

When the alarm chimed at six, he realized his hand was on her hip, and her ass was nestled against his morning wood.

It wasn't like he was mad about it. Although, he realized she might be, so he quickly rolled away to shut off the alarm and get out of bed.

He went into the bathroom to pee, then splashed some water on his face and brushed his teeth before picking up his son and gently shaking Olivia's shoulders to rouse her from her slumber.

She had to be exhausted. Hell, he was tired, and he wasn't even doing that much. He decided she wasn't going anywhere for at least a few more days—she needed her rest. She could order new clothes and have them delivered. Although, he didn't even want her getting out of her pajamas today.

In the meantime, he'd wash what she did have, then lie back down for another hour before making her breakfast.

That had been the plan, anyway.

CHAPTER SEVENTEEN

Maverick

He dreamt that he was a young boy, sitting at his mother's kitchen table while she stood at the stove making a big breakfast. After he ate bacon and eggs, he morphed into a dragon and flew off to find Sawyer and Olivia so they could have breakfast, too.

The smell of bacon pulled him from his slumber. Once he placed the smell, he reached over to Olivia's side of the bed and found it empty, and the sheets cool to the touch.

Been there, done that.

Only judging by the smells wafting into his room, she hadn't gone far this time.

He scrubbed his hand along his chin and groaned when he remembered he was supposed to be the one cooking her breakfast. Glancing at the clock, he sat up with a start. It was half past nine. Why hadn't his alarm gone off?

Making his way to the kitchen, he stopped short when he observed the scene from the doorway.

There she was in his boxers and t-shirt, with her black hair piled high on her head, holding a spatula like a microphone while singing acapella the Ronette's "Be My Baby" to Sawyer, who was wide awake, sitting in his car seat on the kitchen island.

She pirouetted to the frying pan on the stove and pushed the contents around, then shimmied back and continued her serenade.

Maverick leaned against the doorjamb and watched silently with a big smile on his face. He could get used to mornings like this.

She screamed when she noticed him, dropping the spatula in the process.

"Oh my god! You scared me," she chastised as she bent down to pick up the fallen utensil. "You shouldn't sneak up on people like that!"

He pushed off the casing and walked toward her. "I'm sorry. You looked like you were enjoying yourself, so I didn't want to interrupt."

Leaning down, he kissed Sawyer's forehead. "Good morning, buddy. Were you enjoying watching your mama dance around the kitchen?"

"Making a fool of herself," she added from her place back at the stove.

"On the contrary. You were adorable."

She ignored his comment. "Are you hungry? I hope you don't mind—I woke up starving and raided your fridge. I'm making bacon, omelets, and pancakes."

"It smells delicious. And of course I don't mind. This is your place, too. I want you to make yourself at home."

"Speaking of home..."

****

Olivia

"Oh shit!" Maverick jumped up from his seat at the island and headed toward the garage, but stopped in the laundry room. It sounded like he opened the washer lid.

"Do you dry your pajamas?" he called.

She shut the burner on the stove off and walked into the laundry room with a quizzical look. "Yeah, why?"

He held up her bra. "What about this?"

She shook her head and tried not to cringe that he'd washed it.

She must not have done a good job because he said, "I washed everything on the handwash cycle, just to be sure."

"Your washing machine has a handwash cycle?"

Of course it did; he had a freaking Rolls Royce SUV in his garage, for fuck's sake.

"What about these?" He displayed the Stanford sweatshirt and black leggings she'd worn to the hospital.

"The leggings yes, the sweatshirt no."

He slung the sweatshirt on his shoulder on top of her bra and tossed the leggings into the dryer, then shut the door.

With the push of a few buttons, the dryer started and he pulled out a drying rack from a cupboard and carefully situated her clothes on it.

"You've done that before."

"I was in the military for twenty-five years. Of course I have."

They walked back into the kitchen, and she set a plate of food in front of him when he sat down at the island next to where Sawyer was.

"Thank you for washing my clothes. That was really thoughtful."

"Thank you for making me breakfast," he countered as he picked up a fork and placed a napkin in his lap. "This looks great."

She waited for him to take a bite. "How is it?"

"Delicious," he said with a mouthful of food.

Olivia turned back to the stove with a satisfied smile and plated her breakfast. When she sat down in the seat next to him, he stood up, opened a cupboard above the coffee maker, and pulled down a mug.

"Can you have coffee?" he asked.

"I can, but I already had a cup, so I'm going to have orange juice."

She stood and he shook his head. "I got it."

"I can get it."

He gave her a stern look that made her sit back down. "Olivia, I can pour you a glass of juice."

Setting the glass in front of her, he returned to his seat and asked, "Did you shut my alarm off?"

"I thought I'd let you sleep."

"That was thoughtful of you."

Olivia took a drink of juice and set it down with a sly grin as she looked at him out of the corner of her eye. "You'll find

I'm actually a pretty easy person to get along with. An ideal person to share custody and co-parent with."

He wiped his mouth with his napkin. "Or an ideal person to marry and raise a child with."

"Why are you so dead set on getting married?"

"Well, darlin', you disappeared on me once, and had it not been for a blizzard, I might not have ever known I have another son, and he wouldn't have known anything about me. I don't think I have to tell you how I feel about that. Or the idea of another man raising my child."

"No, you don't," she said quietly. "But you know about him now, so that's no longer an issue."

"The issue now is you want me to be a part-time parent, and I'm not interested in that."

"But why married?"

"Call me old-fashioned, sweetheart."

"Even though we'd just be roommates?"

"Who said anything about roommates?"

"We have separate bedrooms."

The corner of his mouth turned up. "But do we?"

Sonofabitch. He'd played her.

Standing abruptly, she announced. "I'm going home."

He took another bite of breakfast and shook his head. "You are home."

****

Maverick

"Why are you being like this? Are you trying to punish me?"

Was he?

Yeah, maybe a little. He still was wrapping his head around the fact that she *meant* to get pregnant. And thought she was going to keep it from him. But he wasn't going to tell her that. And she still hadn't admitted she didn't really have a boyfriend.

"No, you daft woman, I'm trying to take care of you and our son."

She crossed her arms across her chest defiantly.

Fuck, her tits are gorgeous.

"I don't need to be taken care of."

"The fact that you think that only proves my point. Of course you do. You just had my baby two days ago."

She tried to interject. "Women all over the wor—"

"Woman, would you stop being so damn stubborn and just accept my help already?"

Shaking her head, she whispered, "I can't."

He cocked his head. "Give the fictitious boyfriend a rest, would you?"

"It's not that."

"What is it, then? Relying on people doesn't mean you're weak, Olivia. When you rely on the right people, it shows you're smart."

Maverick could tell she was sizing him up, as if trying to determine if he was one of the 'right' people.

"Let me give you a hint, darlin'. I'm someone you want on your side."

CHAPTER EIGHTEEN

Olivia

She didn't go back to her house for several days. Maverick made her take it easy and went out of his way to wait on her.

He made her feel like a princess.

Which made her uncomfortable as hell. She was the person who took care of others, not the other way around.

On the fourth day, she insisted she wanted to go to her house, and he lightened up with his bedrest insistence.

As she got Sawyer dressed in one of the cute outfits Maverick's brothers had bought, Maverick walked into the bedroom.

"You're not planning on taking the baby."

It wasn't a question.

"Well, he's a little young to be left alone, don't you think?" she sassed back.

He shook his head. "I'll be here."

"So how am I supposed to get to my house? I don't have a car here."

"I have a few cars you can choose from, Olivia."

"I'd like *my* car.

She didn't like relying on him so much—having her own transportation was a good start to reestablishing her independence. And moving back into her home.

When he didn't say anything, she grumbled, "I'll just call an Uber."

He gave her an exasperated look as he punched buttons on his phone. She heard his phone alert with a text seconds later.

"Nick will be by in thirty minutes to take you. Can you wait?

Waiting half an hour was not a hardship, so she wasn't sure why she sighed and said, "I guess," like a brat.

If Maverick noticed, he didn't comment. Instead he picked up Sawyer and said, "What should we do while your mommy is gone?" Then he walked out of the room deep in discussion with their five-day old.

**

It was weird walking into her house. She still loved her place, but after having spent the last few days in Maverick's mansion where everything was the best of the best, she couldn't help but notice where her place was lacking.

Not like her home was a shack; she'd been proud of it and always enjoyed having people over. But there was no comparison to where she'd been staying. Even her cats seemed to like it at Maverick's.

But it was just temporary, until she managed to convince him that he really didn't want to live with her, and joint custody would be best for everyone. Maybe once the holidays were over, he'd get on board.

"So, he's treated you like a princess and is a great father... tell me again what the problem is? Why are you objecting to being with the father of your child?" Rose asked when Olivia called her from her car on the way back to Maverick's. She'd wanted to have lunch but had to get back to feed the baby.

"I deserve what you and Chad have. I'm not going to be with a man just because he's not an asshole and it's convenient for me to live in the same house while we raise our child. If I'm going to be with someone, it's going to be because we're in love."

"Okay, I get that. And I totally agree, by the way. You should have it all—love, family, and career. You deserve nothing less."

At least someone got it.

Then he called her into his office when she got back, and she decided that love might have to wait. She had a better idea.

Why she chose to ignore that her last great idea had not gone according to plan would forever remain a mystery.

****

Maverick

"Everything go okay at your place?" he asked when she walked into his study.

"No problems. Nick was really sweet and stayed to load my suitcases into my car for me."

He knew—he'd asked his son to do that.

"He's a good kid," was all Maverick said in reply.

She plopped down into a chair and looked at him with raised eyebrows. "So, what's up?"

"I'm hiring a company to decorate for the holidays and was hoping to get your input. They have a whole catalog of colors, themes, etcetera, and I have no idea when it comes to that stuff."

"You're *hiring* someone? Why? We can put up a tree and some decorations, Pete."

"You're correct, and maybe next year we will. But I don't want you overdoing it, and having professionals come in and do all the heavy lifting while you pick what you want and point where you want it seems like a better alternative. I have a feeling if I were to do it, you'd be inclined to try and help with the manual labor. Whereas if I'm paying someone, you'll be more willing to let them do it."

She considered him with pursed lips then sighed in defeat. "You're not wrong."

That elicited a knowing grin from him.

"Which brings me to the other thing I wanted to talk to you about... The other reason I want this place decorated."

"Other than the holidays?" she quipped.

He slid a folder in front of her.

"What's this?"

He waited until she'd pulled the prenuptial contract out and began reading it.

"I'd like to get married Christmas Eve. Here."

She flipped through the pages, then looked up at him with narrowed eyes.

"You don't hear the word *no* very often, do you?"

He thought about it for a second. "Actually, I don't."

Olivia put the papers back in the folder and closed it, pushing it away from her as she deadpanned, "You don't say."

"Did you even read it?"

"I read the title—I didn't need to go any further."

"You should have your attorney review it, of course, but I think you'll find the terms are in your favor."

Maverick opened the folder and pointed to the bullet points of the contract with the tip of his pen as he read them aloud.

"In the event that *I* divorce *you*, you'll automatically be awarded full custody and given a million dollars for every year we're married, with a minimum of one million, plus monthly child and spousal support. Sawyer will have an irrevocable trust fund, so you won't have to worry about saving for his college. If *you* divorce *me*, you'll leave with what you came into the marriage with, and we'll let a judge decide the custody arrangement."

"How is that any different than if we just went to court now?"

"I think a judge would look more favorably toward you and less favorably toward me if you at least tried to be married to me, but I was so unbearable you couldn't stand it."

His description made her smile briefly, but then he watched her wheels turning.

"So, if you divorce me, you walk away and will only see Sawyer when I allow it?"

He nodded slowly as he noticed her eyes start to flash, as if she was formulating a plot.

"What about my boyfriend? Can I still see him?"

His nostrils flared at the mere mention of her being involved with someone else.

"That would change things, as there's a fidelity clause— for both of us. If I'm unfaithful, it makes the contract null and void, and you'd probably be able to get half my assets in divorce court, plus full custody. If you're unfaithful, then it negates the part of the contract that I won't fight you for custody, and voids your million-dollar-a-year golden parachute, plus spousal support."

"I don't want your money, Pete."

His laugh was mirthless. "Just my baby."

"*Our* baby," she corrected.

"Our baby."

"Why can't we split custody now and bypass all this? We can work out terms that are agreeable to both of us."

"I already told you, Olivia. I'm not missing out on raising my son this time."

She flopped back against her seat in obvious aggravation. "You're such a stubborn ass..."

He raised an eyebrow at her. "Careful, darlin'. I might start to think your mouth is made for dirty things."

Olivia crossed her arms and returned his stare, not backing down.

"I seem to recall you already experienced all the dirty things my mouth is capable of."

A small grin escaped him. "Oh sweetheart, I'll bet that was just the tip of the iceberg."

His sassy little baby mama didn't back down.

"I don't think you gave me the tip of anything that night."

His cock moved at the memory of being balls deep in her. No, there was definitely more than the tip that night.

CHAPTER NINETEEN

Olivia

Whoa, hussy. Quit flirting. That's what got you in trouble in the first place.

But she wouldn't trade her son for anything and had no regrets about that night. Even now, with Maverick insisting he be completely involved or he'd sue for full custody.

She glanced down at the paper in the folder. Maybe this was the answer she'd been looking for. He was willing to put in writing that he'd give her full custody if he divorced her. That seemed easy enough.

"So, is there anything in here about sex between us?"

The corner of Maverick's mouth tipped up. "Why, do you want there to be?"

"No!"

Okay, that might be a lie. She needed to reign her hormones in. Her vagina was in no condition for sex, and sleeping with him could complicate the plan that was forming in her head.

He cocked his head. "So, what do you mean?"

"Does it specify we have to have sex X number of times a week or something?"

He chuckled as he shook his head. "No. There's nothing in there that requires us to have sex. Just no sex with other people."

"So we could be married eighteen years and have a sexless marriage?"

That prospect seemed downright depressing. Especially with the fidelity clause. She liked her battery-operated boyfriend just fine, but the thought of that being her *only* outlet for getting off didn't appeal to her in the least.

"Theoretically. Although, I think I'd be a pretty lousy husband if I let your needs go unattended for a fraction of that long."

She remembered how well he had attended to her needs over nine months ago.

"So you *are* planning on having a physical relationship."

"I'm not *planning* on anything. I just don't see the point of ruling it out, do you?"

"The point is, sex only complicates things—obviously. If I'm going to even consider marrying you that needs to be made clear up front."

His smile was placating. "How about we not put anything in writing and just have a gentleman's agreement that there will be no sex between us unless you decide otherwise?"

"Fine. But I'm not going to change my mind."

He didn't flinch. "Okay," he said dismissively, like it didn't matter to him one way or another. "So, Christmas Eve, then? How many people would you like to invite?"

Was she really going to agree to this?

"Well, first of all, we're not doing anything here. I'm not allowing a slew of germ-infested people anywhere near my son who hasn't gotten any of his shots yet."

"Good point. I hadn't thought about that. What about the country club?"

She wrinkled her nose. "Not if you want to do it this Christmas Eve. I'm sure they're booked and have been for months.

They sat thinking quietly, until finally she suggested, "How about Flannigan's?"

It was his turn to wrinkle his nose. "You want to get married there?"

"Why not? It's where we met. Would Derrick be willing to close that night? I know Christmas Eve can be a busy night for some bars."

He thought about it for a minute, then shook his head. "I'm not marrying you in a bar."

"We could just go to the courthouse."

"I'm not marrying you at the courthouse. either. How about this? We get married here, but keep Sawyer in the bedroom wing—away from everyone, and have professional cleaners come in overnight."

"On Christmas Day?"

"Money talks, Olivia."

"If you can arrange that, I'm on board."

****

Maverick

The decorators came and Olivia was the perfect project manager, choosing decorations and directing the workers, all with Sawyer strapped to her front in a baby sling.

It was a sight to see. He had no doubt she was a force to be reckoned with.

Which was why he was surprised that she had acquiesced so easily to signing the prenup and agreeing to marry him Christmas Eve. He'd expected her to come back from her lawyer's office with all kinds of demands. The only thing that she asked to be changed was two million a year, instead of one, and Maverick suspected that was her attorney's doing. He'd needed to suggest *something* in order to justify his fees.

Maverick easily signed off on that. He didn't give a shit about the money and would have paid her more if she'd asked.

Now his house was filled with silver and blue bulbs, bells, and wreaths. Garland was strung along the banister, and there were three giant Christmas trees throughout.

Three.

One in the foyer, one in the living room, and one in front of the floor-to-ceiling window in the great room where they were going to get married.

Married.

He stopped to think about that. If you would've asked him at Thanksgiving if he'd be married by Christmas, he would have doubled over laughing. Of course, he would have done the same if he'd been asked about having a baby.

Yet here he was.

And he was so in love with that little guy, he worried his heart might burst from his chest when he looked at him.

Then there was his future wife.

That relationship was going to be trickier. She was fiercely independent, which he found sexy as hell. Unfortunately, right now she viewed him as the enemy.

Granted, that was his own doing. If he would have just agreed to a custody arrangement, she might not hate him now.

But fuck that. He was going to be there for all his son's firsts this time. He'd been given another chance to do it right and he wasn't going to squander it.

Olivia would come around. Meanwhile, her alleged boyfriend had not—which was for the best, for everyone.

CHAPTER TWENTY

Olivia

"You're doing what?!" her twin roared into the phone.

"I'm getting married, Evan."

"Over my dead body. I thought he'd given up with that nonsense."

Her family had been to Maverick's multiple times to visit Sawyer. Each time, Maverick had charmed her parents when they came and clashed with Evan when he showed up.

Or should she say, Evan clashed with Maverick. Mav was always the consummate host, and her brother was a boorish guest. Pete didn't talk about marrying Olivia because that seemed to set her brother off, and he bent over backwards to make Evan feel welcome. Her brother, on the other hand, would ask in front of Maverick when she was moving back to her place, or if she needed any help watching Sawyer when she went back to work—knowing full-well that Maverick planned on being a stay-at-home dad.

"He hasn't. It's happening Christmas Eve at our place. Guests arrive at six for cocktail hour, and we'll exchange vows at seven."

"Oh, it's *our* place, now?"

"Well, I do live here."

For now.

"What about your place, Olivia? Please tell me you're not selling it. You're going to want someplace to go when this thing blows up."

While she'd been thinking the exact same thing, she didn't need to hear it from Evan. She was going to put on the happy wife façade for everyone until after the wedding, when she made Maverick miserable enough to divorce her.

So her big brother needed to shut the hell up and let her do her thing.

There was a method to her madness.

"I haven't decided what I'm going to do with it. Pete said he'd make the mortgage payment until I figure it out."

Her plan was to be back in it by March first, right around when she went back to work.

Getting him to divorce her should be easy enough. Living with him, she'd already honed in on his weaknesses. After they said, 'I do,' on Christmas Eve, she'd exploit them, and soon he'd be begging his lawyers to draw up the divorce papers.

Not that she planned on keeping Sawyer from him once their marriage ended. He really was an awesome dad. They were just going to have to work out the schedule they should have in place already. And it was going to be on *her* terms.

"Anyway. You and Hope are welcome Christmas Eve. I know it's last minute, so if you already have plans and can't make it, I totally understand.

"Like I'm going to fucking miss my twin sister's wedding. Even if it's bullshit, and we both know it is."

"Can't you just wish me well like everyone else?"

"Well, I'm not everyone else—I know you, and this is not what you want, so no, I can't just pretend this is awesome news. It'd be different if you loved him, Liv."

I like him. Does that count?

Evan was making the same argument she'd had with herself, and with Maverick.

Unfortunately, Evan wasn't done. "If you can look me in the eye the next time I see you and tell me you love him, then I'll shut my mouth forever and wish you nothing but the best."

"Promise?"

"I'll know if you're lying, Ollie."

He was trying to bait her. The fact that he called her by that annoying nickname was proof.

"If you're going to cause trouble, tell me now so I can uninvite you. Your girlfriend can still come, of course."

"I am going on the record that I think this is a huge mistake, but if you still choose to go through with it, I will be on my best behavior."

"Noted, and thank you. I'll see you next week."

Since it was such short notice, Maverick went to the trouble of having their guests' invitations hand delivered. It was a small list, less than fifty people total. He invited his family: his brothers, Nick, his parents, and Nash—even making arrangements to fly his mom, dad, and son from Florida on a private jet once Olivia voiced her concern about them being around Sawyer after flying on a commercial plane.

Nash was only going to be there for two days, since that was the most time away the Navy would give him, but his parents were going to be in town for a week.

He also asked his other business partners, while she only invited her immediate family, and Rose and Chad. Maverick asked her if she wanted to invite her office staff or any other friends, but she declined.

"The fewer people I have to explain to that my husband divorced me, the easier it will be."

He raised an eyebrow at her. "Not happenin', darlin'."

Olivia tried to disguise her smirk. "We'll see."

**

Rose sat on the sofa in the dress shop, drinking champagne while Olivia tried on wedding gowns.

"So, he turned out to be Prince Charming after all?" her friend called from her seat.

Olivia poked her head out from behind the changing room curtain. "What do you mean?"

"Last time we talked you didn't even want to live with him; said you deserved the fairytale and implied he couldn't give that to you. Now you're marrying him?"

She gulped. "I kissed the right frog, I guess."

Except, the only kiss he'd given her was on her forehead, like he did their son. Still, Rose didn't need to know that. Not yet, anyway.

Olivia zipped up the winter white, floor-length Italian wrap dress, then stepped out.

Her friend let out a small gasp when she saw her. "Oh, Liv, that's the one. You look gorgeous."

Olivia stepped onto the small platform in front of three mirrors that let her see the dress from all angles. It was off the shoulder, with a slit up the leg, and cinched at the waist with a ruffle along the side to help disguise her post-pregnancy body.

"I don't know about gorgeous," she said as she turned to check out her backside in her reflection. "But I think you're right. This is the one."

"Maverick isn't going to be able to keep his hands to himself when he sees you in it."

She doubted that. They'd slept in the same bed every night since she moved in, and he hadn't seemed the least bit interested.

Still, she laughed like Rose was right.

She wasn't sure why she felt the need to keep her marital situation a secret—especially from her brother and best friend. Maybe she didn't want them judging her, or worse, tell her she was making a mistake. Not when she worried enough about that herself; the last thing she needed was someone close to her confirming it.

After keeping Sawyer's paternity a secret for almost her entire pregnancy, pretending she was a blushing bride should be a piece of cake.

When Olivia came out of the dressing room in her street clothes, Rose wrapped her arm through Olivia's and murmured conspiratorially. "Now let's find the perfect shoes and some sexy lingerie for your wedding night."

****

Maverick

Olivia had left a bottle of breast milk while she went wedding dress shopping and to lunch with her business partner.

And little Sawyer wanted nothing to do with the silicone nipple.

"I don't blame you, buddy. This is nothing like the real thing," he murmured as his son turned his head to reject the bottle while becoming increasingly agitated the hungrier he got.

"Come on, little man. If you eat, you'll feel better," Maverick pleaded when the baby screamed bloody murder.

He was *this* close to calling Olivia and begging her to come home, when he heard the garage door open. He'd moved his Porsche into the car barn so Olivia would have a stall for her car.

He wanted to buy her a new Mercedes as a wedding gift, but when he'd asked her what model she'd like, she told him that was frivolous and her car was perfectly fine.

His future bride was not marrying him for his money, of that he had no doubt.

No, she was marrying him to guarantee she didn't lose custody of the red-faced, screeching child he was bouncing in his arms as he met her in the kitchen.

"Oh, sweet boy!" she crooned patiently as she set her purse and shopping bags on the counter, then moved to the sink to wash her hands before taking Sawyer from Maverick. In one movement, she pulled her sweater and bra down to expose her breast, and their starving child was quickly silenced as she nursed in the armchair in the small sitting area by the bay window in the kitchen.

"He wouldn't take the bottle, huh?"

"No. No matter what I did, he wanted nothing to do with it."

"That's pretty normal. We'll work on it."

"Either that or you're never leaving this house for longer than three hours at a time again."

She laughed like he was joking.

He wasn't.

He gestured to the bags on the counter. "Did you get a dress?"

Her face lit up. "I did."

"I can't wait to see it."

She cocked her head. "Really?"

His brows furrowed. How could she ask that? "Of course. I'm sure you're going to be stunning."

She stared at him a minute longer, then drew her attention back to their son. Her hair was piled on her head, but it was starting to fall loose around her face as she stared down at Sawyer. There was such love in her eyes for their little boy, Maverick's solar plexus tightened as he watched them.

He knew she was going to be a knockout when she walked down the makeshift aisle in their great room on Christmas Eve, but he had a hard time believing she could be any more beautiful than she was at that moment.

She glanced up and gave him a soft smile when she found him staring.

With a cough, he looked away.

"I'm going to make some lunch. Are you hungry?"

"Starving. We didn't have time to eat."

"Why?" he asked with a frown as he pulled a pan from the cupboard. "You should have gone to lunch with your girlfriend. It was probably nice to get out."

"It was. But I had a feeling he wasn't going to take the bottle."

"Well, selfishly, I'm grateful and relieved that you cut your afternoon short. He was a hangry little guy. But I also feel bad that you had to." He winked as he turned on the burner. "I'll make it up to you."

She looked up at him with hooded eyes. "How?"

By making you scream my name as I make you come.

He couldn't tell if she was flirting with him, so he kept that thought to himself. He remembered Patricia had no interest in sex after she had Nick and Nash.

Still, he gave her a cheeky grin. "I'm sure I'll think of something."

149

She raised her eyebrows at him and murmured, "I'm sure you will."

That time, he definitely knew she was flirting.

After she finished feeding and burping Sawyer, she laid him on the ottoman and changed his diaper in a matter of minutes. Maverick was still getting the diaper thing figured out.

"You're amazing, you know," he said as he set her plate in front of her when she sat down at the table.

"What?"

He tilted his chin toward Sawyer, who was in a milk coma in her lap. "With him. You make it look so easy."

"You understand part of my job is to help bring these guys into the world, right?"

"I do. I just didn't think that included feeding them and changing diapers."

"That's true," she conceded. "But it happens more than you think."

They ate in silence for a few minutes before she said softly, "You're pretty great with him, too." Then a grin escaped her lips. "Diaper changing and bottle feeding aside, he's calm when he's around you—that says something."

"Oh? Like what?"

"That he inherently knows he can trust you to keep him safe."

He made sure to look her in the eye when he replied, "I'll keep you both safe."

Olivia

She was a strong, independent woman. That statement should not make her toes curl.

But it did.

Partly because she didn't doubt it for a second.

Pete was inherently a good man. If she needed more proof than the fact that he was marrying her so he could be with his son, in their week of living together, not only had he taken care of her and Sawyer, but he'd made sure his other sons were doing okay. He'd been especially worried about how Nash was taking the news of being an older brother and had reached out to his ex-wife to ask her to check on him.

Even her traitorous cats seemed to like him better. Oscar could often be found lounging in Maverick's office with him. The feline spent so much time in there that Maverick moved the cat tree into the corner next to the window. Now both Honey and Oscar spent their days watching out the window and following Maverick around the house like he'd invented salmon cat treats.

Maverick seemed to be the guy everyone counted on. His phone rang constantly throughout the day. She lost count of how many fires he put out without ever breaking a sweat. He always kept his calm demeanor that seemed to be comforting to everyone around him.

Even his sweet *abuela* housekeeper, Juanita relied on him.

She'd come into the house the day before with pink cheeks and shaky hands, and immediately sought him out. They'd been in his office, Maverick working at his computer while Sawyer slept in his baby bouncer on the floor next to his desk, and Olivia read her Kindle in a chair by the fire.

"Mr. Maverick," she'd said urgently, her Mexican accent heavier than when Olivia had met her a few days before. She was obviously upset about something. She glanced at Olivia and offered, "*Buenos días*, Miss Olivia," without waiting for a reply before continuing. "There's something wrong with my car. I couldn't stop, and I hit your bushes."

He jumped up and went around his desk to examine the older woman. "Are you okay?"

"*Si*, but your bushes are not."

Maverick waved his hand dismissively. "I don't like those damn things, anyway."

He then spent the afternoon in his car garage replacing her brakes. And of course, refused to accept a dime.

"I'll make you a cheesecake," Juanita said when he wouldn't even entertain letting her buy the parts.

"And enchiladas?" he asked hopefully.

She beamed proudly. "Of course."

At dinner, Olivia understood why he'd requested her enchiladas. They were the best she'd ever had. And the woman's cheesecake was to die for.

"How often does she come?" she asked.

"Right now, twice a week—mostly just to cook and do laundry for me, but with the cat hair and the extra laundry, I think I'll ask if she can come three, maybe four times a week."

Olivia thought about arguing, saying it wasn't necessary—she could do the extra work, but the truth was, not having to worry about cooking and cleaning was appealing enough to make her pride shut the hell up and accept the help.

Especially since Maverick wasn't technically the one doing it. Just the one paying for it. A technicality, but a loophole for her ego nonetheless.

CHAPTER TWENTY-ONE

Maverick

Christmas Eve morning arrived and once again, he woke with his arm wrapped around her waist, and her ass nestled against his hard cock.

It was a good thing she usually slept soundly in the three hours between feedings, because he often woke up like this. Normally, he'd casually roll away, careful not to wake her, but since it was their wedding day he decided to lay there for a few minutes and enjoy the softness of her curves against his hard planes.

He breathed her familiar floral scent in deeply, closing his eyes as he let it wash over him. He was marrying this gorgeous woman in a few short hours. How the hell did that happen?

Oh yeah, she'd tricked him in order to get pregnant.

And he was so glad she did.

He decided to savor holding her just a little longer. When she started to stir, he reluctantly rolled away and slipped out of bed before she felt his cock poking her.

"Good morning," she called softly as he walked across the floor.

"Good morning."

He glanced back at her lying in his bed. She looked like a siren beckoning him back to bed as she rubbed the sleep from her eyes while her tousled hair cascaded down her shoulders. Maverick had to will himself to keep walking.

"Merry Christmas Eve."

"Happy wedding day," he countered.

"Is that today?" she teased with a twinkle in her eye.

Maverick couldn't help but smile. "Tomorrow you'll wake up a married woman." He paused at the threshold of the bathroom and turned around with his hand on the casing. "Have you decided if you're going to change your last name to Mitchell?"

He definitely wasn't doing that hyphenated shit his brother had talked to him about.

She smoothed the comforter at her sides. "Um, I think it would make sense professionally if I didn't. I've worked hard to build my reputation; I don't want to lose that."

A pang of disappointment hit his stomach. Call him a caveman, but he wanted her to take his name.

"Can you keep your maiden name for your practice, but legally change it for everything else?" He quickly added, "That way you and Sawyer have the same last name."

She glanced over at the still-sleeping boy and said wistfully, "That's true. But I don't know if I'd still be able to go by Lacroix professionally if I legally change it. To be honest, I hadn't thought about it until you mentioned it."

He'd thought about it, and may have done a little research on the matter.

"I think Massachusetts gives you a month after the wedding to decide."

She tilted her head. "How would you know something like that?"

Busted.

"I was married before, remember?"

Her face fell, and she made pouty lips. "Aw."

"Aw?"

"Your next wife is going to be number three. Well, you know what they say, third time's a charm."

"I'm not divorcing you, Olivia." He smirked then turned on his heel and threw, "I can't afford it," over his shoulder before disappearing into the bathroom.

He was pretty sure he heard her mumble, "We'll see about that," before he shut the door.

****

Olivia

Her parents showed up late that morning bearing gifts. Not wedding presents, but more toys, books, and clothes for Sawyer. Like he didn't have more than enough between her baby shower and Maverick's brothers' shopping spree.

They did, however, bring a little tuxedo onesie with black pants and socks.

"That is so adorable," she exclaimed when she pulled it from the bag as they relaxed on the comfy chairs in the sitting area of the kitchen.

Maverick walked in from the garage, his phone wedged between his shoulder and ear when he looked over at them. Olivia held up the outfit, and he broke out into a wide grin.

Covering the mouthpiece, he whisper-shouted, "My little mini-me," then continued toward his office.

That assessment wasn't far off. She was beginning to see a lot of the Mitchell genes in her son.

"You remember he's not coming tonight, though, right? Maverick's housekeeper, Juanita, is taking care of him."

"I know, but it was so cute I couldn't resist. Maybe you can take a family photo after the ceremony."

That sounded like a sweet idea. Probably the only one they'd take as a family. It'd be good for Sawyer to have when he got older.

Jack and Judy bickered over who got to hold him as more and more people started to arrive. The caterers and the florist were the first to get there, followed by the valet company, photographer, and string quartet. Other than offering her opinion when he asked, Olivia had been out of the wedding planning loop. Maverick had taken care of everything.

How he thought he was going to plan a wedding in two and a half weeks—and on Christmas Eve, no less—had left her shaking her head.

"There are a lot of people who owe me favors," had been his cryptic reply. "I've got everything under control; the only thing you need to worry about is your dress."

She'd shrugged and done just that. The beauty of it not being a real marriage had allowed her not to stress. If everything worked out, great. If not, she wouldn't be upset.

Judging by the steady buzz of people circulating through the house, he'd pulled it off without a hitch.

Of course he had.

Was there anything he couldn't do?

Apart from stay married to her, that is.

CHAPTER TWENTY-TWO

Maverick

The wedding planner who'd charged him a ridiculously exorbitant rate had turned out to be worth her weight in gold. Things were running like clockwork, so when his parents arrived with Nash, he was able to break away.

Greeting his now-middle child with a warm hug, he beamed. "I'm so glad you could be here."

"So, where's my soon-to-be stepmom and baby bro?"

He led them to the kitchen, where he'd last seen her.

Olivia was nowhere to be found, but her parents were still seated in the butter-leather chairs by the window.

"Jack, Judy, I'd like to introduce you to my mom and dad, Henry and Sandra."

The grandparents exchanged pleasantries and seemed to hit it off. There was a noticeable chill in the air when he mentioned that his parents were staying with them for a week.

He tried easing the tension. "Jack and Judy, you're still coming tomorrow for Christmas, right? You'll both have plenty of grandbaby time then."

"We call dibs on watching him when you go on your honeymoon," his mom said with a saccharine-sweet smile.

"Watching a baby isn't like calling shotgun, Mother," he said as he leaned down to kiss her cheek.

"Speaking of Sawyer, when do we get to meet our new grandson and future daughter-in-law?"

"Olivia took him upstairs to nurse and then try to get a little rest before she needed to get ready," Judy explained.

He turned to the group. "I'll go see how she's doing."

Taking the stairs two at a time, he slowly opened the door of their bedroom suite and slipped in quietly, in case she was sleeping.

The curtains were drawn, so it took a minute for his eyes to adjust to the darkness in the room.

"Hey," her soft voice called from the bed. "Is it time already?"

Maverick sat down next to her on the bed.

"That depends—how long do you need to get ready?"

"Probably an hour and a half, if I factor in time to nurse."

"Then you still have an hour before you need to get up."

She turned on her side to face him, hugging a pillow as she did. "Good. I'm pooped, and I haven't even had to do anything yet."

"Except take care of our three-week old son and entertain guests."

"I'd hardly call my parents guests."

He shrugged. "Did you have to entertain them?"

"Well, kind of. Although, I'm currently taking a nap so I'm not sure how good of a job I did."

"They are perfectly content in our kitchen. Full disclosure, my parents and Nash are there with them."

She threw the comforter off her. "Oh, I need to meet them!"

He covered her back up.

"You'll have plenty of time after the wedding."

"With your parents, but not with Nash."

"We have all day tomorrow. You need to nap. Tonight is going to be busy."

"I can't sleep."

I bet a good orgasm would knock you out.

But he knew that was out of the question—her body was still healing.

"What can I do?"

Her voice was small when she asked, "Can you lay with me for a little while? I sleep better knowing you'll take care of Sawyer if he wakes up and I don't have to be hypervigilant."

He'd already kicked off his shoes and was climbing into bed before she finished her request.

She nestled against him like a little spoon, a position that felt all too familiar. Maybe he wasn't the guilty party after all when it came to waking up with his arm wrapped around her and his cock pressed against her ass.

Like it was doing right now.

"Sorry, darlin'," he murmured in her ear. "You have that effect on me."

"It's okay. I know it's just biology."

"No, sweetheart," he growled as his hand caressed her belly over her blouse. "It's chemistry."

****

Olivia

It was a testament to how tired she really was that she was able to doze off after that.

CHAPTER TWENTY-THREE

Olivia

Her breath hitched when she caught sight of Maverick waiting by the Christmas tree in the huge family room with the soaring ceiling and wall of windows facing the snow-covered back yard. It was a picture-perfect scene.

And the man could rock a tux like nobody's business.

His eyes twinkled when their gaze locked, a small smile on his lips as she walked down the short aisle to where he was waiting for her.

"You're stunning," he murmured in her ear as he took her hand.

"You don't look so bad yourself," she whispered back.

She found herself smiling as they turned to face the officiant.

Thankfully, the ceremony moved quickly, and when it got to the part where they were supposed to exchange rings, she panicked. She hadn't gotten him a ring!

He must have sensed her dismay because he winked at her and mouthed, "I've got it."

Of course he did.

Reciting, "With this ring, I thee wed," he slid a platinum eternity band on her finger. It was simple and sophisticated, and would be perfect to wear to work.

Except I'm not going to still be married when I go back to work, she reminded herself.

Then he put an oval diamond ring on her finger that almost blinded her. It had to be three carats, easy. And while it was completely impractical, she had to admit it was stunning.

"It's beautiful," she said quietly.

He winked at her with a soft smile, then fished a platinum band from his pocket and handed it to her to put on his finger, addressing the crowd as he did.

"She took care of the baby, I did the ring shopping."

That elicited a low laugh before she also repeated, "With this ring, I thee wed," and put the band on his left ring finger.

Thank goodness they hadn't said anything about the rings being a symbol of their love for one another. She wasn't sure she'd be able to handle hearing him lie.

Loving their kid wasn't the same as loving each other. Sure, they liked one another, but unfortunately, that was soon going to change.

He just didn't know it yet.

CHAPTER TWENTY-FOUR

Maverick

Their house was joyously busy on Christmas Day.

His mom made a huge breakfast, and his older boys appeared at the table with bedhead, wearing pajama pants and sweatshirts with the word NAVY written across them.

Maverick had played Santa and put presents under the tree for everyone after they'd all gone to bed.

It'd seemed like old times, only he appreciated that his kids weren't up at the crack of dawn to see if Santa had come. He probably had a few more years before that started again.

It was nice having his parents in town. They'd welcomed Olivia with open arms, as had Nash. Maverick had a feeling Nick liking Olivia as much as he did had gone a long way in influencing his younger son's opinion of his new wife.

The night before, Olivia had been as charming with their wedding guests as she was beautiful. All three of his brothers tripped over themselves to attend to anything she needed.

Derrick made sure she had sparkling cider for the toast, since she wasn't drinking yet because she was breastfeeding. Beau heard her mention she'd set her phone somewhere and couldn't find it, and made it his quest to locate it. And Gabe sought the caterers out and made sure they got her a hot plate of food when she came back from feeding Sawyer.

Meanwhile, Maverick congratulated himself—repeatedly—for marrying her. Seeing his ring on her finger while she animatedly waved her hands around when she talked made him want to beat his chest, drag her upstairs, and do what newly married people were supposed to do.

All night.

Even if by some miracle she wanted to, knowing they couldn't, since she hadn't gotten the okay from Rose, had him settle for a kiss on her cheek before they went to bed.

The only one who seemed immune to her charms was Evan.

Her brother had a perma-scowl on his face the entire night, as if someone had pissed in his cornflakes that morning. Hope even had to pinch him and tell him to smile when they posed for photos with her family.

If Olivia was bothered by her twin's attitude, she didn't show it. She continued flitting about like the perfect hostess. Maverick was so fucking proud to be with her.

Thank God he'd decided to have dinner and watch the Bruins that night at Flannigan's, and she had come in for a cheeseburger after work, not realizing the hockey game was on. If she'd known, would she have stopped in?

Then they felt the sparks between them, went across the street, and made their little boy.

And nine months later, his oldest son drove her to the hospital?

How was that *not* divine intervention? They were supposed to be together. Maybe they were doing things out of order, but they'd get on track. They had to.

****

Olivia

Her parents joined them for Christmas dinner, along with Maverick's three brothers and two adult sons. The long table in the formal dining room she'd thought was unnecessarily and obnoxiously gigantic proved to work out perfectly.

They ate early so Nash could make his flight back to Florida. As she watched father and son embrace in the doorway, her eyes teared up. The love between them was obvious, and both were emotional about him leaving.

That gave her a sense of peace about the relationship Sawyer was going to have with his dad. Even though Nash's mom was married to someone else, the two were still close. Olivia wasn't going to have to be the one to teach her son how to be a good man—he'd have a role model for that.

CHAPTER TWENTY-FIVE

Olivia

"You're cleared to have sex," Rose said as pulled off her blue gloves. "Although, I'm kind of shocked to hear that you haven't already."

"Of course we haven't."

Rose looked at her with furrowed brows, so Olivia quickly added, "I know better than that."

"After watching you two make googly eyes at each other all night at your wedding, I thought for sure you were going to risk it."

She'd gotten so caught up in the romance of that night, she'd almost thought so, too. Especially after the exchange they'd had in bed before the wedding. Then he came into the bedroom while she was nursing Sawyer, kissed her cheek, changed out of his tux and into his pajama pants, and got into bed—careful to stay on his side once she joined him.

Although she should have known he wasn't interested in anything more after the chaste kiss he'd given her once the officiant proclaimed them husband and wife, and the equally innocuous kisses they exchanged whenever someone tapped their glass at dinner.

Olivia had felt so rejected she didn't even snuggle up next to him once he'd fallen asleep.

The night she'd arrived they'd wound up spooning. She didn't know who had initiated it. But when she woke up nestled against him with his strong arm around her, she realized how safe he made her feel, so she'd started doing it regularly. Once his breathing slowed and evened out, indicating he was asleep, she'd scooch her back to his front to be the little spoon.

She reasoned she could always claim ignorance if she got caught. Sleep snuggling—kind of like sleep walking, only different. But so far he'd just gently pushed her away when he woke up.

"He's been a patient gentleman," Olivia said with a polite smile as she stared at her feet hanging from the exam table. She really needed a pedicure.

"What are you guys doing tonight for New Year's?"

"We don't have any plans. His parents left yesterday, so I think we're staying in and just having a relaxing night. What about you and Chad?"

"You know he won't go out on New Year's Eve. Sometimes being married to a cop can be a real killjoy. I took the on-call shift. Let someone who'll celebrate it right have a chance to go out."

That made Olivia giggle.

Rose stood from her rolling stool. "We're done. Go ahead and get dressed—you know the drill. Let's have lunch on Saturday? Noon at Flannigan's? Celebrate New Year's a day late."

"Yeah, I'd love to."

"Great! I'll see you then. I want to hear all about your reunion sex."

"Ohmygod!"

"As your best friend, not as your doctor."

"Duh."

She was going to have to read some erotica to get ideas for the lie she was going to have to tell.

Of course, she had better stop by her house and pick up her battery-operated boyfriend if she was going to do that.

And she really needed to commence tactics to get him to divorce her.

****

Maverick

He waited in Olivia's office with Sawyer while Olivia had her four-week checkup.

He heard the rapid clicking of heels coming down the hall and knew it was Rose before she even popped her head in the doorway.

"How's my godson? I heard he got his shots today."

They'd gone to Sawyer's appointment before coming here for hers.

"He did. He's not feeling that great."

She pulled the baby from his car seat and bounced him in her arms.

"Aw, poor little guy. Did that mean pediatrician poke you with a needle?"

"I don't know who was more upset, me or him."

"It doesn't get easier. Chad was just as traumatized with our fourth as he was our first."

"I'm not sure we're even going to have a second, let alone a fourth."

Rose smiled smugly. "Well, she's been given the all-clear, in case you want to start practicing."

"Oh, uh, that's great!"

On one hand, it really was great news, and his dick might have moved at the thought of the new possibilities. On the other, now he couldn't blame her not wanting him on any physical limitations.

Olivia appeared a few minutes later, and they said their goodbyes and headed home.

"How'd it go? Everything okay?" he asked as he maneuvered the Cullinan through the Boston streets.

"Yeah, everything's fine."

She didn't mention she'd been given the okay for sex. Although, he wasn't exactly sure how she'd casually interject that into the conversation.

"I, um, can start working out again."

That was a start.

"Oh yeah? No limitations?"

"No. No limitations."

He glanced at her, then back at the road. "So, do you want to work out with me?"

Translated—do you want to have hot and sweaty sex?

He looked over at her again when she didn't answer right away.

Finally, she said, "I checked out your... gym. It's impressive."

Was she talking about his home gym or his cock?

"I have no doubt it can satisfy your needs."

"I think I might be intimidated working out with you. I want to try it by myself first."

"Are you sure? I'll go nice and slow. Ease you back into it."

He definitely was not talking about the gym.

"Thanks. It would have to be nice and slow. I haven't, um, worked out since... well, it's been a while."

Fuck subtlety. And these metaphors were getting annoying.

"I haven't worked out since Sawyer was conceived."

"That was the last time I did, too."

He smirked. "You didn't work out with your boyfriend?"

"No. He—" She paused, then simply said, "No," again without offering any further explanation.

"Well, the offer's there. Should you want to get some exercise."

"Thank you. I've been thinking I might be in the mood to do just that."

"I'm a great workout buddy."

"Buddy... yeah."

****

Olivia

She didn't know what to think about Maverick offering to be her fuck buddy.

Granted, she had been feeling more like her old self lately, and sleeping next to the muscular, shirtless man every night had made her well-aware of her healed female parts, while watching him with Sawyer had been doing things to her heart.

Yet, did she want to be fuck buddies with her husband? The man she'd planned on divorcing sooner rather than later? It seemed like a bad idea.

But the fidelity clause of their prenup, not to mention her own morals, meant he was her only option if she wanted any kind of physical intimacy with a three-dimensional man and not a vibrating penis substitute. And she knew first-hand how good Maverick was in bed.

What to do, what to do?

She decided her best option was to do nothing.

"Do you want to get takeout for lunch?"

CHAPTER TWENTY-SIX

Maverick

He thought he'd been making inroads with her, then she did an about face and asked about lunch.

He could practically hear the *womp womp* of the soundtrack to his sex life.

But they were married, he didn't need to rush things. He was playing the long game.

"Yeah, takeout sounds good. What did you have in mind?"

She surprised him by suggesting they order from a local pizzeria, specifically, their "Pizza, wings, and breadsticks special."

He gave her an inquisitive look. "That's a special?"

"Well, I'm not sure if it still is. It's been a while since I've been there. But it was a staple in my and Evan's diet when we were in high school. We both worked there our senior year."

"Sounds good. It should tide us over until later tonight. Juanita is making us a New Year's Eve dinner."

They ended up eating in the family room together while Sawyer slept. He'd been cranky since getting his shots that morning, so it was a relief that he didn't wake up when they brought him in from the car.

"Poor baby," Olivia said when she put him on the floor next to the couch "First your parents starve you this morning, then they made you get poked with needles."

Their latest attempt at getting him to take a bottle had been that morning, and they'd been wildly unsuccessful.

"Thanks for going today," she said as she opened the food boxes on the coffee table.

"Of course. I told you, I don't want to miss anything this time."

"I'm glad we found you again. You're a great dad. Sawyer's lucky to have you."

It sounded like a compliment, but there was something about her demeanor that seemed sad.

That was the only reason he didn't throw in a dig about lying to him that she was on birth control.

"Thanks. That means a lot. I'm glad you found me, too."

****

Olivia

Sawyer was happier when he woke from his nap, and Maverick took him from his seat and the two had an animated discussion as they sat on the couch together.

The baby watched his dad's face carefully and broke out into his first smile, mirroring Maverick's. He kicked his legs excitedly and let out a happy squeal.

Olivia's heart was a pile of goo at the sight.

She'd meant it when she told him she was glad they'd found him again. Sawyer's life was going to be infinitely better having his father in his life.

Which was why it was more important than ever to get him to divorce her. Before she fell head over heels in love with him.

Although part of her worried it was too late, and that was why she'd been dragging her feet putting her plan into action.

CHAPTER TWENTY-SEVEN

Maverick

He and Olivia spent New Year's Eve night like an old married couple, playing card games in the sitting area of the kitchen while they ate the traditional New Year's Mexican food Juanita prepared for them—*Ensalada de Noche Buena*, tamales, pozole, and mole. Then they watched the Times Square ball drop as it rang in the New Year. They clinked their champagne flutes filled with sparkling cider, and he leaned down to kiss her.

After all, it was customary, right?

He'd intended for it to be chaste, like he'd done at their wedding, but when he put his hand on her hip there was desire in her hazel eyes as she looked up at him, and he couldn't help himself.

"Happy New Year," he murmured, his lips inches from hers.

"Happy New Year." Her voice was a husky whisper.

The kiss started gently. Her lips were soft when he captured them with his. Then she fucking whimpered and grabbed his shirt like it was the only thing keeping her upright, and all bets were off.

Maverick snaked his hand around her waist and tugged her tight against him as his tongue sought hers out. Part of him expected her to slam on the brakes, so he was pleasantly surprised when her tongue dueled with his for control.

Angling his mouth to deepen the kiss, he quickly established he was in charge.

Olivia shamelessly ground her hips against his erection. He thought he might bust a nut right then.

He broke the kiss. Breathing heavily, he dropped his forehead against hers and looked into her eyes.

"Are you sure about this?"

She nodded quickly.

He closed his eyes tight and groaned when he remembered, "I don't have any condoms."

Rubbing his cock over his pants, she whispered, "We don't need any."

That made him raise an eyebrow. Did she want another baby already?

Maverick couldn't help but grin. "Where have I heard that before?" He was teasing, of course. She had no reason to lie now.

She rolled her eyes. "Breastfeeding is an effective method of birth control. For the first six months, anyway."

He kissed the spot on her neck just below her ear and was rewarded when her body broke out in goosebumps.

"Just so you know, darlin'," he murmured in her ear, "if you do want another one, I'm all in."

"How about we just practice for now?" she said with a smug smile.

He grabbed her hand and kissed her knuckles. "You know what they say, practice makes perfect."

He tugged her toward the stairs, and she pulled away, so only the tips of their fingers were touching.

"I think it will be weird with him in the room."

He didn't need her to explain who she meant by 'him'.

He grabbed the baby monitor on the kitchen counter they'd been using. "Let's go in the guest room, then."

Quick, before she changed her mind.

****

Olivia

"Are there any rules?" he asked as he reached behind his neck and pulled his shirt over his head.

"Rules?"

She didn't move to undress, preferring to watch him instead. He remedied that by unbuttoning her blouse for her.

"Yeah, rules." Pulling her shirt open, he stared at her heavy boobs in her unsexy nursing bra. "Like, am I allowed to kiss and lick your nipples?"

That made her giggle nervously. "Um, I don't mind, but you do so at your own risk."

He softly traced her skin along the edge of her bra.

"I'm not afraid of a little milk, darlin'."

"Well, fair warning, I can't guarantee it will only be a little."

"Fair warning back, I'm okay with that. What about your pussy? Am I allowed to lick that?"

She closed her eyes and smiled, remembering the last time he'd eaten her pussy. "Mmm. Allowed and encouraged."

Glancing down at his fingertips caressing her skin, she swallowed hard.

"Actually, I do have a couple of rules."

"Okay..."

"You have to go slow."

"Obviously."

"And... the lights need to be off."

He walked to the light switch, but instead of flipping it to off, he only moved the dimmer down.

"I can't agree to off, sweetheart. If I'm going to properly worship your beautiful body, I need to see it."

She winced at the thought of him seeing her stretch marks and post-pregnancy belly.

"You're not hiding your body from me, Olivia."

"But..." Her voice got smaller. "I don't like how I look."

"I do. Your body is incredible. My son grew inside it. You're fucking gorgeous."

Before she could protest any further, he reached down to unbutton her jeans.

"Stop arguing, woman, and get naked so I can put my face between your sexy thighs."

"Well, when you put it like that..."

****

Maverick

His mouth watered as she lay naked on the guest bed with her legs spread wide. He'd dreamt of her taste for the last ten months, and finally he was going to experience it again, for real.

With the first swipe of his tongue, she arched her back off the bed.

He lifted his head and asked, "You good?"

Placing her hands in his hair, she drew his mouth back to her center.

"So good."

He couldn't fight his grin. That's what he liked to hear. "Say red if you want me to stop."

Maverick leisurely explored her folds with his tongue, relishing her taste along with every sexy sound she made.

Slowly, he screwed a finger inside and glanced up to watch her reaction.

"Still good?"

With her eyes closed, she whimpered, "Uh huh."

"Is that a 'it feels good' uh-huh, or a 'that hurts' uh-huh?"

"So fucking good. Please shut up and keep going. I'll say red if I want you to stop."

He chuckled.

Well, okay then.

His tongue zeroed in on her magic button, and he worked his mouth and finger in rhythm until she was chanting instructions.

"Pete! Yes! Just like that!"

"Don't stop! God, don't stop!"

And finally, after he quickened the pace, just a repetition of his name until she erupted in spasms as the orgasm racked through her body while she stuttered, "Ohhhhh fuuuckkkk!"

He kept going until she squeezed his head between her thighs and giggled, "Mercy! Mercy!"

Maverick climbed up alongside her body and lay next to her, elbow bent with his head resting on his hand while he studied her.

"Oh my god," she panted as she stared at the ceiling, hand on her stomach. "You're as amazing as I remember. I didn't make it up."

"You're as delicious as I remember."

Olivia pulled his face to hers and kissed his mouth.

"Let's see if you're as good with your cock as I remember."

She didn't have to ask him twice.

****

Olivia

She lay with her hair fanned out on his chest while he absent-mindedly traced circles on her hip.

"As good as you remembered?" he asked as he kissed her head.

"Mmm, better." Nuzzling closer, she purred, "So much better."

"Promise me you won't leave in the middle of the night this time. Or, if you do, at least not with my kid."

Ouch.

Olivia whispered her reassurance. "I'm not leaving."

"Good. I think we make a good team."

"Me, too."

He might as well have thrown ice water on her instead of his next remark. "And I'm glad we're workout buddies again."

She didn't even know how to respond to that. That's what this was to him?

Fortunately, Sawyer's cries came through the monitor, and she jumped out of bed. "I need to get cleaned up."

"Take your time, I'll get him."

Chapter Twenty-Eight

Maverick

His son had impeccable timing.

He'd waited until Maverick had come deep inside Olivia before deciding to wake up and cry.

"Thanks for giving your mommy and me some uninterrupted grownup time, little man," Maverick whispered as he pulled the hungry baby from the bassinet. Olivia had disappeared into the bathroom to clean up while he went to console the inconsolable infant.

"You know, you're going to have to take a bottle pretty soon," he told the sobbing boy. "If you'd just cooperate, you wouldn't be so dependent on your mom, then she could go do things."

Olivia reappeared in the middle of his conversation and snatched Sawyer from his arms, defensively sniffing, "There's nothing wrong with depending on his mother."

"Of course not. But if he started taking the bottle it would free you from being tethered to him all the time. You could actually have an afternoon to yourself to go shopping, or maybe a spa day and lunch with your girlfriends, whatever you wanted—without having to rush home to nurse him."

"It's okay. I don't mind being 'tethered.'"

She made an air quote with one hand as she offered her boob to their son with the other.

He groaned internally. They'd just finished consummating their marriage not more than five minutes ago, and he'd already pissed her off.

"I didn't mean to offend you. I just thought you'd like a break."

Her shoulders visibly relaxed and her expression softened.

"You're right, I'm sorry. I'm probably just being sensitive because I know my time with him is going to come to an end soon, and I'm not ready for that."

"You've got, what, three months before you have to go back to work?"

"Two and a half," she corrected. "That's going to fly by in no time. He's already a month old."

"Have you thought about quitting?"

She jerked her head back like he'd slapped her. "I couldn't do that to Rose or my patients."

Maverick held his hands up in a surrender gesture. "I was just asking. What about working part-time?"

She chewed on the inside of her bottom lip, something she often did when something was troubling her.

"It's never been an option, so I've never considered it."

He shrugged. "Something to think about. You have choices. Not that I'm not looking forward to time with my little man."

"Yeah, I'll think about it.

****

Olivia

Damn him and his soft lips. They'd lured her into having sex with him. As if watching him care for their son, then falling sleeping next to him every night, hadn't been enough to make her feelings for him grow, throw in her crazy hormones and now mind-blowing sex. It'd been easy to fool herself into thinking it meant more than it did.

Fortunately, he'd been sure to let her know it didn't mean anything more to him than a WWB situation. Wife with Benefits.

She obviously didn't tell Maverick that it wasn't an option for her to only go back to work part-time. Not if she was going to be a single mother, as originally planned.

Even if she really did get the two million the prenup awarded her, raising kids was expensive—she knew that wouldn't be enough to quit her practice. Besides, she had never really counted on her 'golden parachute,' as he liked to call it. She knew how those things worked. He'd take her to court and fight her over the terms, and her attorneys' fees would wind up costing more than it was worth.

He had, however, made a good case for staying married to him—maybe at least until Sawyer started school. It wasn't like she was miserable living there, and they did like each other.

But she knew her traitorous heart couldn't handle just being his fuck buddy. No matter how great the sex was, it wouldn't make up for the fact that he was only with her because they had a child together.

"I deserve the fairytale," she whispered to herself.

So no, she wasn't settling.

CHAPTER TWENTY-NINE

Maverick

They didn't talk about what transpired between them New Year's Eve night, something he knew was a big mistake. But the more time that went by, the harder it was for him to broach the subject with her.

So he followed her lead and pretended like it hadn't happened.

As they sat in the living room a week later with the TV on while neither of them really watched it, there was a palpable chill in the air.

She stared out the window at the snow starting to come down, then stood and walked to the heavy drapes that were rarely closed and bent down to retrieve something from behind the curtain.

Waving a blue glass ornament when she stood, she said, "They missed one."

The decorating company had come that week and removed all remnants of the holidays. It had been bittersweet. While Maverick liked the idea of a clean slate that came with the new year, the house had been so festive, and he was sad to see it go.

"It feels kind of bare in here now, huh?"

She sat back on the couch and looked out the window again. "Yeah. I wish once the holidays were over we could just skip to spring. Either that, or I need to start skiing again.

"We could rent a chalet in Vermont for a weekend and hit the slopes."

She shook her head. "Maybe next year."

"Let's plan on it," he replied with a cheery smile.

When she didn't respond, he picked up the shiny decoration she'd set on the coffee table and twirled it in his hand. "I think next year we should decorate the weekend after Thanksgiving—whether we hire someone or do it ourselves."

"They did a beautiful job," was all she said.

He was desperate to keep the conversation going. "It was nice letting someone else handle everything—especially the cleanup."

"That's usually the part I dread the most."

"Me, too. The only thing I'd do differently is have a tree just for us to decorate with family decorations."

Her smile was tight. "Yeah."

The doorbell rang, and he checked his phone to view the camera at the front door.

"It looks like we have a delivery. Did you order something?"

She looked toward the ceiling, as if trying to remember. "No. I haven't bought anything online."

Disappearing to retrieve the package, he came back in holding a box, and after looking at the return address, announced, "It's from my parents."

"I hope they didn't send more clothes or toys. They gave him so much while they were here. He's going to outgrow half the outfits before he has a chance to wear them."

That was true. The drawers his brothers had bought were filled to the brim, with overflow on the shelves in the nursery closet.

"Let's find out." He took his folding knife from his pocket and cut the tape that sealed the package closed.

A wide grin spread across his face when he looked inside. It was perfect.

He held it up, and she offered another one of the polite smiles she had perfected in the last week.

It was a crystal picture frame with a photo of the three of them: Maverick in his tux, Olivia in her gown, and Sawyer in his tuxedo onesie. His mom had followed the two of them when they slipped away after the ceremony to check on Sawyer and snapped the photo. He hadn't thought to ask for a copy.

They hadn't gotten the professional photographer shots from the wedding back yet. They'd taken some of just the two of them, then the usual poses with his family, then hers, and finally, the entire group. They'd taken some in in the upstairs foyer so Sawyer could be included in some, but Maverick didn't remember posing for any with just the three of them. He was grateful to have his mom's photo.

He expected Olivia to want to look at it closer, but she didn't say anything other than, "That was nice of your parents."

Maverick looked down at the photo—his new little family. "Yeah, it was." Tracing his son's cheek over the glass, he murmured, "I sure do love that little guy."

****

Olivia

She was thrilled that Maverick loved Sawyer as much as she did—really. What made her stomach drop to her feet was when she realized where she fit in the equation.

Technically yes, she was his wife, but in reality, she was nothing more than Sawyer's mom that he had to live with in order to be with his son. Oh, and an occasional fuck buddy.

Seeing the picture of the three of them had felt like karma biting her in the ass for using deceit to get pregnant. She should have paid the money and used a sperm donor. Or been more patient and found the right guy to fall in love with and have his baby.

Instead, she was in love with the wrong guy—her husband.

She needed to move into her own bedroom. Sleeping in the same room every night like they were a real couple was messing with her head.

And the plan to get him to file for divorce was about to go into full effect. Enough stalling. He wasn't going to magically fall in love with her—the sooner she accepted that, the better off she'd be.

CHAPTER THIRTY

Maverick

"Everything okay?" he asked when she came to breakfast holding Sawyer at her shoulder, still dressed in her pajamas. Other than Christmas Day, she'd always come down showered and dressed.

But ever since she moved into her own bedroom and Sawyer into the nursery, she'd become even more distant. He blamed it on their lack of spooning.

"Yeah," she said flatly. "Why?"

"No reason. It just feels like you've been upset with me for a while."

She pulled a mug from the cupboard with one hand, then popped a coffee pod into the new machine he'd bought and pressed start.

Leaning against the counter, she asked with wide eyes, "Why would I be upset with you?"

He was convinced that question was a trap; being married to Patricia for fifteen years had taught him a thing or two. He'd been racking his brain for weeks trying to figure out what he'd done to make her mad.

"I don't know. That's what I've been trying to figure out."

She walked to the pantry and pulled out the sugar bowl, passing him as she did.

"Nope. Everything's fine."

"Great, I love it when things are *fine*," he muttered under his breath, then said loud enough for her to hear, "Well, if you realize things aren't fine, and you want to talk about it, I'll be in my office. Do you want me to take Sawyer?"

She observed him with narrowed eyes, like he was some stranger planning on running off with her baby. Finally, she handed their son to him.

"He might need to be changed."

Maverick lifted the little guy's bottom to his nose and quickly put him back down, wincing as he turned his head to try and escape the smell.

"Whew. That would be an affirmative."

Her smile was sickly sweet as she spooned sugar into her coffee mug and slowly stirred. "Thanks for taking care of that. If we were divorced, you wouldn't have to."

Divorced, my ass.

He noticed she set the wet spoon on the counter and shuffled away without a second thought. She also left a pile of sugar next to her spoon, same as she'd done the day before. Now that he thought about it, she'd been leaving a trail of messes the last few days. He was smart enough to keep his mouth shut about it. Even if he did almost break his neck tripping over her shoes strewn about the hall.

As he stepped over a pile of dirty baby clothes in Sawyer's room, however, he decided to talk to Juanita about coming more than three days a week.

CHAPTER THIRTY-ONE

Olivia

She was in the kitchen making a sandwich while Sawyer slept in his crib in the nursery when she heard Maverick come through the door leading to the garage.

"Did you mess with the tools in my toolbox and workbench in the garage?"

Her back was to him, so she was able to disguise her smirk before slowly turning around.

"I needed a screwdriver."

"You needed a screwdriver," he repeated.

"Uh huh."

"For what?"

"Oh, um, a knob on Sawyer's dresser was loose."

"So, you had to rearrange all my tools in the process?"

Oh, did I do that?

"I couldn't find what I was looking for."

His tone was dripping with annoyance. "The drawer marked 'screwdrivers' wasn't obvious enough for you?"

This was the first time her antics had gotten under his skin, and lord knew she'd been trying. She didn't know why it hadn't occurred to her sooner to mess with his workspace in the garage.

It had been so orderly, it had been painful for her to fuck with it. Kind of like leaving the messes she'd been making all week. Not picking up after herself went against the very nature of her being, and her hands actually twitched each time she'd walked away and left things dirty. But she knew it would bother Mr. Military Man more, so she'd made herself do it.

"Huh. I guess I missed that."

His jaw was clenched as he stared at her for a long beat, and finally he snarled, "Did you?" like he knew what she was up to.

"Yes," she said with as much innocence as she could muster.

"Really? Because I have cameras in the garage..."

Oh fuck.

Her heart rate skyrocketed to the point it was making a whooshing sound in her ears, but she tried to look unaffected as he continued. "And that's not at all what it looked like happened. It looked like you deliberately rearranged my tools."

He took an ominous step toward her.

"And I asked myself, 'Why would my wife purposefully try to piss me off?' For the life of me, I couldn't think of an answer. So rather than make assumptions, I thought I'd do you the courtesy of coming to the source and asking for an explanation."

He took more slow, methodical steps until he loomed over her. The calm tone in his voice was even more scary than if he'd yelled at her—which was what she'd prepared herself for.

Although, looking at it now, it was dumb of her to think he'd respond that way, since she'd lived with him for almost six weeks and had yet to see him be anything but cool and collected. Even when he was operating on four hours sleep.

"I—I don't know what you're talking about. I was simply looking for a screwdriver. I don't know why you'd think I was doing anything but."

She'd read somewhere that if you're going to lie, you gotta commit to it. Plus, she had no idea how else to respond.

He cocked his head. "If I didn't know any better, I'd think you were looking to get punished."

Punished!?

"Excuse me? You think you're going to punish me? Like I'm a child?"

His hand slid around her neck and he forced her to look at him as he crooned, "Yes and no. Yes, I'm going to punish you, but no, it won't be anything like a child."

"And you think I'm just going to allow this to happen?"

He squeezed her throat subtly and leaned down to whisper in her ear, "Yes."

Well, *that* wasn't what she'd expected.

And why had her heartbeat suddenly moved from her ears to her pussy?

"Dream on bud—"

In one quick movement, he threw her over his shoulder and gave her a firm smack on her ass, then marched through the house, up the stairs, and to the owner's suite.

Unceremoniously dumping her on the bed, he barked, "Strip."

"You've got to be kid—"

He ripped her shirt down the middle without warning. "Take. Your. Fucking. Clothes. Off. Now."

She was so turned on. While she'd seen a hint of his dominance the night she'd gotten pregnant, she'd almost forgotten about this side of him. He'd been such a kind and patient man since he brought her home.

Still, she defiantly raised her chin at him.

"Make me."

The corner of his mouth hitched, and she knew she was in trouble—in the best kind of way.

"Gladly."

****

Maverick

While he'd been at Flannigan's that morning meeting with Derrick, the garage camera alerted that someone was at his workbench. Glancing at his phone, he saw it was Olivia, so he returned to the conversation with his brother without a second thought.

Pulling into the garage, he noticed his neat and orderly workspace was anything but neat and orderly.

He got out of his truck and walked to the empty stall he used for his workshop. It looked like a tornado had blown through his six by four foot tool chest. Drawers were left open. Hammers were where the screwdrivers should be. Wrenches were with the pliers. He couldn't even find his tape measures. Nothing was where it belonged.

But it didn't stop there. Moving on to his workbench, he discovered his tools that had their own specific space on the pegboard were in disarray: his saws out of order, the levels moved haphazardly around. Not even the bins of screws, nails, and bolts had been spared.

Dumbfounded and confused, Maverick logged into the security system to review what the hell had happened.

It didn't make any sense. The only alerts he'd gotten were when Olivia had been in the garage. Had she fallen? Tripped? Had a seizure? Even those scenarios didn't explain the mess his space was in.

When the video started to play, he couldn't believe what he saw. His beautiful wife, the mother of his young son, had willfully and deliberately fucked with his shit—and with a smile on her face as she did it.

She was obviously pissed off at him and had been acting passive-aggressively for the last few weeks, leaving little messes everywhere she went. He'd been a dumbass, and rather than address it head-on, had chosen to ignore it.

Apparently, his new bride didn't like being ignored and had decided to go next-level to get his attention.

Well, he was going to pay attention to her, alright. She was about to get the brattiness fucked right out of her.

When her eyes dilated as he ripped her blouse, he knew that was exactly what she needed.

Her sassy "Make me," comment told him he was on the right track.

He yanked her yoga pants and panties past her ankles, dispatching them to the floor before pulling her legs apart to find her pink center glistening.

"Your pussy's soaked, darlin'," he said with a smirk as he ran his finger down her wet slit. "If you wanted me to fuck you again, you could've just asked. You didn't need to destroy my workspace."

"Please." She rolled her eyes. "It was hardly destroyed, and no, I don't want you to fuck me again."

Maverick plunged a finger inside her.

"You sure about that?" he taunted as he methodically finger-fucked her.

"Positive."

The sound from her wet pussy echoing off the wall suggested otherwise.

"Just like you didn't deliberately fuck with my things to get a rise out of me?" He added a second finger and circled her clit with his thumb. "Tell me, sweetheart, was this the reaction you were hoping for?"

"No."

"No?" He unzipped his pants and pulled his cock out, thrusting it inside her with no pleasantries. "Then this must be what you wanted."

It's what I wanted.

"You're delusional," she snarled, while at the same time arching her back and moving her hips to meet his thrusts.

He stopped moving. "So this isn't what you want?"

Maverick knew it was a risky move. She was stubborn and proud, and making her admit that she wanted him might backfire.

"Did I say red?" she sassed with a glint in her eye.

He couldn't help but smirk as he pushed his cock deeper into her pussy. "No, darlin', you did not."

****

Olivia

Having him throw her over his shoulder like a caveman, rip her shirt, and fuck her had not been the goal.

The goal had been to piss him off enough that he'd realize he couldn't live with her and demand a divorce.

But as he plunged his cock in and out of her needy pussy, driving pleasure deeper with every thrust, she decided this unexpected turn of events was an acceptable alternative.

She'd fantasized about having a boyfriend shove her against a wall and fuck her senseless to remind her he was in charge, but no one she'd ever been with had *really* been the boss. But oh. My. God. His thick cock slamming in and out of her, causing shivers to dance through her system, was showing her exactly who was the boss. Her commanding new husband.

He flipped her onto stomach and smacked her ass again, and she liked it. Hell, she wanted *more*.

"My naughty, *naughty* wife." He emphasized each word with blows to alternating cheeks. "You. Make. My. Cock. So. Fucking. Hard."

"What are you going to do about it?" she challenged over her shoulder, her forearms on the comforter.

"Fuck you. Hard."

Oh, she was hoping he'd say that.

"So, what are you waiting for?"

"You need to beg me, darlin. Beg me to fuck you."

****

Maverick

Her whispered plea was barely audible—another act of defiance, he was certain, so he jerked her head back by her hair.

"I can't hear you."

"Please fuck me," she moaned.

Maverick was more than happy to oblige.

Pushing inside, he asked, "You still good, darlin'?"

"Yessss," she hissed.

He fucked her faster, his balls slapping against her as he delivered a round of slaps to her ass. The sight of her pink flesh jiggling under his hand made his cock even harder, if that were possible.

Maverick felt a tingling sensation shoot up his spine and knew he needed to stop, or he was going to come before she did, and that wasn't going to fly. Forcing himself to close his eyes didn't work. Her pussy was too warm and inviting.

Pulling out, he buried his face between her thighs, inhaling her delicious aroma before tongue-fucking her. while his fingers found her swollen clit.

With her face on the mattress, she pushed back against his mouth while moaning her approval of his ministrations.

He replaced his tongue with two fingers so he could talk dirty to her.

"You like being punished, don't you?

"Yes," she panted as she spread her knees wider.

He could feel her getting wetter as her pussy gripped his fingers. Maverick amped up the pressure on her clit.

"Are you going to come for me, naughty girl?"

"Mmm hmm," she whimpered.

"That's it," he demanded. "Come on my fingers like my naughty little slut."

Her body went taut, her pussy clenched so tight around his fingers he couldn't move them, then she cried, "Oh my god," as her body spasmed.

It was sexy as hell.

When the last twitch of her orgasm subsided, he pressed his cock into her entrance, his climax not far behind hers. He pumped into her, pleasure rushing through him in a dizzying wave.

Holding her hips tight as he roared his release, he felt her pussy quiver around his dick as she came again.

He dropped his forehead to her back while he caught his breath.

"I think that was the hottest sex I've ever had," she purred under him.

"Me too, darlin'."

He knew the night he met Olivia that she had a bratty, submissive streak; he just hadn't seen it again—until today. He liked it. A lot. And he looked forward to exploring it with her for, say, the next fifty years.

CHAPTER THIRTY-TWO

Maverick

Things went back to semi-normal once they got out of bed. He was happy to note that she picked up her shoes as she walked down the hall.

After nursing the baby, she brought him downstairs, where Maverick promptly took him, and father and son sat on the couch together to have a spirited conversation.

Olivia watched from the other end of the couch, her eyes smiling as she took another video. Between the two of them, they'd acquired more pictures and video of their six-week-old son than Maverick's parents probably took throughout his entire childhood.

When Sawyer let out a happy squeal and flailed his arms and legs, they both laughed out loud and beamed proudly, like their son had just ended world hunger.

Soon he dozed off again and Maverick laid him down on the quilt she'd spread on the floor.

The cats came by to sniff him, like they did on occasion, but quickly opted to sit on the back of the couch and bat Olivia's hair that she'd put up in a messy bun.

"You guys are weird," Maverick said to the felines.

"They really are. At first I thought they were glad to be sleeping with me again, but I think they've secretly been plotting my demise so they can have the room all to themselves once more."

"That's not going to be a problem."

She tilted her head. "It's not?"

"I mean, I thought... after this afternoon, you'd want to sleep in our room again."

He was careful not to call it *his* room.

"I'm not sure that's a good idea."

Maverick's jaw clenched. When he realized what he was doing, he consciously relaxed and tried to remain calm when he asked, "Why not?"

"Sharing a bedroom makes things blurry."

Blurry? What the fuck did that mean?

"I need more information, darlin'."

"It just is confusing."

No, what's confusing is you.

"I don't understand. What exactly is confusing?"

"Us. If we're sleeping in the same bed, it's like we're a couple."

He rubbed the corner of his eyebrow, trying to mask his frustration. "Uh, we're married. How much more of a couple could we be?"

"You know what I mean. We're married, but we're not *married*."

What the fuck is she talking about?

"What would make us *married*?"

"I don't know. If we were in love and wanted to be together, not because we wanted to avoid a custody battle."

He'd thought they'd worked past that.

"Oh.

She tucked her legs under her and sat up straighter. "Let me ask you this—if it wasn't for Sawyer, do you think we'd be together?"

"Well, no. You took off in the middle of the night without leaving me a way to get in touch with you."

He could tell by her expression that wasn't the answer she wanted, so he tried to do damage control. "If you hadn't wanted to get pregnant, would you have gone to a hotel room with me that night?"

She thought about it for a second then shook her head. "No, probably not. I don't make a habit of having one-night stands."

"I don't, either, and yet, we both did that night. And we got a beautiful baby boy out of it. So, it doesn't matter whether we'd be together if we didn't have him. We *do* have him, and that's what counts."

****

Olivia

How fucking romantic.

He'd hurt her feelings with his answer. She knew it was stupid, but she'd wanted him to say they would have been together no matter what. Just like the universe had brought them together for Sawyer, it would have found a way to bring them together.

His stupid, practical reply felt like rejection to her vulnerable ego—that was the only reason she could think of why she lashed out.

"If only I'd waited a few more months. I would have had the love of my life's baby."

Maverick pursed his lips as he deliberated what she'd said. Finally, he spoke. "The love of your life, huh? The one who never even came to to the hospital? I think you dodged a bullet, sweetheart."

"How could he visit me when you were standing guard the whole time?"

"Like I said, if you were my girlfriend, nothing would have stopped me from being there."

Except I'm your wife, and you couldn't care less.

CHAPTER THIRTY-THREE

Maverick

They were back to being distant roommates, but at least she wasn't passive-aggressive this time. In fact, they both seemed to go out of their way to be accommodating to one another.

Unfortunately, there were no repeat trips to Orgasm Town. He suspected that was part of the reason she'd been so cooperative, so he wouldn't throw her over his shoulder again like a Neanderthal.

Although, he knew damn well she'd liked it. At least, at the time. But, just like New Year's Eve, she seemed to instantly regret it once they were dressed again. Maybe she really did have a boyfriend and felt guilty for being with Maverick?

That would explain a lot.

He sat down to eat the lunch Juanita had prepared for them.

"Can I ask you something?"

Sawyer was asleep in the baby sling on her chest. "Sure."

"What's your boyfriend's name?"

She narrowed her eyes at him. "Why?"

"I'm not going to seek him out, if that's what you're worried about. I'm just curious."

"Well, considering I'm married to you, he's no longer my boyfriend."

"What's your *ex*-boyfriend's name?"

"My ex's name?"

It was his turn to look at her suspiciously. In his experience, anytime someone repeated a question, it was so they could stall for time to think of a lie.

"Yeah. What's his name."

"Casey Montoya."

"Do you talk to him anymore?"

"Again, I'm married to you, what would be the point?"

"So, if you weren't married to me, would you still be with him?"

"Would I still be with him if I weren't married to you?"

Again with the repeating of his question.

"Yeah, say there hadn't been a blizzard and you hadn't needed Nick to drive you to the hospital... would you still be with him?"

"That's really hard to say. I mean, Sawyer is my sole focus right now."

"So, no?"

"I, um, I'm not sure."

"You said you guys didn't sleep together."

"I did?"

"Yeah, you told me that you hadn't been with anyone while you were pregnant."

"Oh, well, that's true."

She was acting too cagey—things weren't adding up. It didn't go unnoticed that she hadn't answered the question about whether she was still in contact with the guy.

Before he could ask any more questions, she tilted her head. "Where is this coming from?"

"I was just curious."

"Now? Why?"

"Something you said the other day. About if had you just been more patient—"

She cut him off. "Oh. I was tired; I should have never said that."

"Usually when your defenses are down is when you tell the truth."

"I'm not lying. I'm not in contact with my ex. I didn't sleep with him while I was pregnant. You and I have an agreement, Pete. I'm not going to be unfaithful, if that's what you're worried about."

He believed she wouldn't cheat, but that didn't mean her heart wasn't elsewhere. He needed to fix that.

"Would you like to go out to dinner with me tonight? Maybe your parents could watch Sawyer."

****

Olivia

Go out to dinner with him?

"Like, on a date?" she blurted out.

"Yeah, I guess. Is it still called a date if we're married?"

"Yes, it's still called that."

"Then I guess I'm asking you out on a date."

He'd rattled her with his line of questioning about her 'boyfriend.' She'd technically told the truth. Casey Montoya was her ex, and they hadn't slept together while she was pregnant. She just failed to mention it'd been almost two years since they broke up. Then he took a sharp left and asked her to dinner. What was going on?

"Why?"

"I don't follow. Why what?"

"Why are you asking me out?"

"Because you're my wife, and we haven't really done anything together that didn't involve Sawyer. I thought maybe we should change that. And you definitely need to get out of the house."

"But you said yourself the whole reason we're together is because of our son. What's the point of us going out without him?"

The corner of his mouth hitched. "Because we're grownups, Olivia, and we need some grownup time away from him."

She felt her spine stiffen. She couldn't sleep with Maverick again. She'd never been good at keeping sex and feelings separate.

"What do you mean, *grownup time*?"

He shrugged. "Time with other adults. Having a conversation that doesn't involve feeding schedules or changing diapers. Maybe even have a cocktail or two. Sawyer's taking a bottle now, and there's enough breastmilk in the fridge that he'll be fine if you want to imbibe."

A martini did sound amazing. It'd been almost a year since she'd had one.

Even though she was leery of his intentions, she found herself saying, "I'll call my mom."

"If your parents can't watch him, I'm sure Nick would. Or one of my brothers. Well, probably not Derrick, since he's always at Flannigan's on the weekends."

"*Every* weekend?"

"He works six days a week."

"Wow, that doesn't leave him time for a social life."

He chuckled. "The bar *is* his social life."

"Okay, then not much time for dating."

He stared at her for a beat. "I think when the right woman comes along, he'll make time."

****

Maverick

Her parents showed up at five. After giving them a rundown of Sawyer's schedule, Olivia disappeared to the guest suite. Jack and Judy were in grandparent heaven as Sawyer blew raspberries at them and had them convinced he was going to roll over with his rocking motion as he lay on the quilt on the family room floor.

"Not yet," Maverick told them. "Liv says probably not for another month or two."

"But our grandson is brilliant," Judy said with a big, animated smile on her face as she looked down at the toothless baby. "Yes, you are. You're going to do everything early, just like your mama did, aren't you?"

Sawyer kicked his feet and arms in agreement.

At precisely six o'clock, Olivia walked through the doorway wearing a black dress and strappy heels. Her hair was curled, and she'd gone to the trouble to put on makeup.

Holy shit, my wife is a knockout.

He couldn't take his eyes off her ruby red lips. An image of them wrapped around his cock sprang into his mind and his dick jumped in his pants.

Down boy.

He wanted her to fall in love with him. Having sex with her while she was still hung up on her ex was part of the reason they were barely on speaking terms.

"You look beautiful, Olivia," her mom gushed. "Maverick, doesn't she look beautiful?"

All he could do was nod stupidly with his mouth hanging open.

Finally, he came to his senses, swallowed hard, and vocalized his agreement. "You look stunning."

She smiled shyly at the floor as she tucked her hair behind her ear. "Thank you. You look very handsome, as well."

Maverick had chosen a pair of grey slacks and a cobalt-blue button down that he'd left open at the neck and rolled the sleeves to his elbows. He'd switched the TAG Heuer watch he wore every day for the Rolex he wore on special occasions. His first date with his wife qualified as a momentous event.

He liked looking at the platinum band on his hand, but even more, he liked seeing the diamond ring on Olivia's left ring finger.

Olivia slipped a black wrap around her shoulders and picked up a black purse. "Are you ready?"

"I am." He swept his hand in front of him and thought he'd test the waters. "After you, Mrs. Mitchell."

She strutted by him with a smug smile. "That's *Dr.* Mitchell, thank you very much."

He'd take it.

CHAPTER THIRTY-FOUR

Olivia

She watched him maneuver the Rolls through the streets with ease. She'd never been into arm porn, until she met Pete "Maverick" Mitchell. His rolled-up sleeves and the heavy watch on his muscular arm ticked her boxes.

Dammit.

She knew she should look away, but she couldn't. Everything about this man made her a glutton for punishment, because everything about him made her get butterflies she was unable to ignore. He'd been drop dead gorgeous in his tux on their wedding day, and tonight, dressed up, he was every bit as handsome. But it was the everyday things that were doing her in. Like when he had his reading glasses on the end of his nose and would look over at her with a crooked smile, or he was concentrating with a pencil tucked behind his ear, or, lord have mercy, when he had on a pair of work boots and jeans. And of course when he held their son.

She needed to get it together.

He interrupted her swoonfest by asking, "Are you really thinking about changing your name?"

"Even if I was, I missed the deadline."

"I think it's easy enough to still do. You'd just have to go before a judge."

Her first thought was, 'okay,' then her inner voice—the one that was trying to protect her—shouted, 'why would I go to all the trouble of changing my name when I'm just going to change it back once we get divorced? Changing all my legal documents sounds like a pain in the ass in the first place, no way am I doing it twice.'

"I don't think it's a big deal, do you?"

He glanced at her, then back at the road a few times before replying, "Well, yeah, I do. My last name is Mitchell, Sawyer's last name is Mitchell. You're part of our family— your last name should be Mitchell, too."

She smiled, even though his words felt like stab wounds to her heart. He was a man who wanted his son and married her to ensure it happened. They weren't some happy family. He didn't love her; she'd best remember that.

"Let me think about it."

**

He'd chosen Frank's Chophouse, one of the best restaurants in the city. The valet took his keys and Maverick escorted her inside.

A man behind the podium looked up at them with a big smile and came around to shake his hand. "Mav! I thought that was your reservation! How the hell are you?"

Maverick responded to the welcome with equal enthusiasm, clapping the man's shoulder with his free hand while smiling brightly.

"Good to see you, Frank." He turned to Olivia. "This is my wife, Dr. Olivia Lacroix. Liv, this is Frank Symanski. He's the owner."

"Thanks to this guy," Frank gushed, then took Olivia's hand. "It's great to meet you. You married a good man!"

She nodded with a smile, then glanced over at her husband. "I certainly did."

"Come on, let me show you to your table."

Maverick put his hand on the small of Olivia's back and they followed Frank to a corner booth.

"Our best table," the man proclaimed proudly.

"Thanks, Frank," Maverick said as he slid in next to Olivia. "The place looks great."

"We've come a long way, huh?"

"That you have."

"Couldn't have done it without you, Mav. What are you drinking? Your drinks are on me, tonight."

Maverick shook his head, "That's not necessary."

"I insist. It's the least I can do, after everything you did for me and my business."

"Thanks." He turned to Olivia. "You feel like wine or a cocktail? Or both?"

Frank interjected. "I've got a beautiful bottle of red you have to try with your meal."

She loved how hands-on Frank was with his restaurant. "How about a dirty martini right now and the wine with dinner?"

"Vodka or gin?"

"Gin, please."

"You got it." He drew his attention back to Maverick. "Mav? Still drinking Johnnie Walker Blue?"

That brought a smile to her husband's face. "You remembered."

"Of course. I'll send your waiter over right away."

"We're not in a rush," Maverick told the man before he whisked away.

Olivia turned in her seat to face Maverick head-on.

"Of course you know the owner of one of the best restaurants in the city. And by the sounds of it, you're a co-owner."

"Actually, I just loaned Frank the money when he first got started, which he paid back long ago. He had grand visions of what his business was going to do and didn't want to sell any of his interest in it." He looked around the crowded restaurant with a grin. "Which is a shame."

"I think you're doing just fine without it," she teased.

"We're not hurting." He winked then went quiet as their drinks were served.

After the waiter walked away, he picked up his rocks glass filled with the amber liquid and clinked it against hers. "Cheers."

Swallowing, he set his glass on the table. "I've been meaning to ask you, have you given any more thought to just starting back part-time?"

She hadn't. Because she knew she'd be tempted, and that would make her dependent on him, which she didn't want to be.

"Have you given any more thought to a divorce?"

He jerked his head back. "Of course not. Why?"

Taking a sip from her martini glass, she shrugged. "Just wondering."

****

Maverick

It hit him like a ton of bricks.

She was serious.

His toolbox, the messes she'd left everywhere, why she hadn't rented her house out or changed her name... she didn't want to be married to him.

He honestly thought after living with him for a while she'd come around. He'd tried showing her how comfortable her life would be with him, that he'd be a good husband. But he realized he hadn't been making progress with her. He'd been making the opposite of progress.

They'd gone from sleeping in the same bed and getting along to sleeping in separate rooms and acting like strangers. Although he appreciated she was back to at least being civil.

None of what he'd done had mattered. She didn't want to be with him. The boyfriend probably really was real.

The thought of her being miserable with him for even one more day bothered him. Still, he wasn't going to miss out on raising Sawyer.

"I can get the paperwork started tomorrow, but I'd prefer you didn't move out until you go back to work. When you do go back, I'll take care of Sawyer while you're at the hospital. I can work around your schedule. Your place isn't that far, and we should be able to make it work. In the meantime, I'd like to call a truce."

Tears of relief immediately filled her eyes. "Okay. I'd like a truce."

He forced himself to smile. "And let's try to have a nice night."

CHAPTER THIRTY-FIVE

Olivia

He was giving her what she wanted, so why did tears spring to her eyes when he told her he'd get the paperwork started, and why did it feel like she'd swallowed a bag of rocks?

Because by giving in, he was confirming what she already knew. He didn't love her.

But it was good—in just six short weeks, she could get on with her life. In the meantime, she was going to do her damnedest to get along with him, like he suggested.

Their conversation at dinner was friendly. Maverick suggesting a truce, coupled with the bottle of delicious red wine Frank had sent over, plus the cocktails when they first arrived, seemed to put them both at ease with each other.

That was why when he suggested they go dancing instead of going home, she thought it sounded like an excellent idea.

"That sounds fun. I didn't know you danced."

"I don't. But I thought I should at least once with my wife while she's still my wife."

The pang that their time together was really coming to an end hit her solar plexus.

"Oh. Well, it'll be fun."

Famous last words.

Turned out, being in his arms as he guided her across the dance floor was bittersweet torture. With his right hand firmly planted on her hip while their left hands intertwined, making the sparkle of her diamond occasionally catch her eye, it was easy to let go and pretend they were a couple in love. Add in the warmth of his body next to hers and the smell of his cologne... even without the alcohol, she didn't stand a chance. And with the alcohol? Well, things were going to get interesting.

****

Maverick

When she laid her head on his shoulder, he couldn't help but wrap his hand around her waist and pull her tighter against him.

"You really do look stunning tonight," he murmured against her hair.

An older couple glided by, and the woman looked at them with a smile. "You make a lovely couple."

Yeah, don't we? he wanted to lash out. Instead, he nodded his acknowledgement while Olivia murmured her thanks.

She looked up at him with a soft smile, and he found himself lowering his face to gently kiss her lips.

Knowing their relationship now had an expiration date must have helped lower her walls, because she returned the kiss without hesitation.

The song ended, but the kiss did not. They were in their own little bubble and Maverick didn't want it to burst.

Slowly, the rest of the world came back into focus, and she broke the kiss. Rather than let her go, however, he continued to hold her tight as he rested his forehead against hers.

"I like when we're in a truce."

"Me, too," she whispered softly.

****

Olivia

They held hands as they walked out of the bar to the valet stand. After Maverick gave the man his ticket, he noticed her shivering under her wrap and pulled her into his embrace. She didn't think she could ever get enough of his masculine scent.

His SUV quickly appeared, and he helped her in the passenger seat, then came around to meet the valet at the driver's door, tipping him before he slid behind the wheel.

The clock on the dash read 11:05.

"Where to next?"

His question surprised her. She'd been under the impression they were going to go home and consummate their truce.

"Oh, um... I'm not sure? We could go to Flannigan's, I guess?"

"We could stop in there for a nightcap."

"We probably shouldn't stay too long, though. I'm sure my parents are already asleep on the couch."

"I told them they were welcome to stay in the guest room."

"Yeah, but they didn't bring an overnight bag or anything, so they won't."

"I didn't think about that. Let's skip Flannigan's tonight. Maybe next time Sawyer can stay at their house."

"Next time?"

He reached for her hand and brought her knuckles to his lips. "We have a whole month and a half left on our ceasefire. I think we should take advantage of that."

"That's true. We should."

They pulled into the long drive leading to his beautiful home.

"I really have enjoyed living here."

"I've enjoyed having you here."

A tiny part of her expected him to revert back to insisting she stay. Maybe even hoped for it?

She gave herself an internal shake. No, that was stupid.

The only reason this so-called truce of theirs was working was because they'd put an expiration date on their relationship. She didn't understand the psychology of it, but was sure there was a name for it.

Six weeks was going to go by in the blink of an eye, and she could move on with her life. In the meantime, she was going to enjoy pretending they were *married* married. It might be the only time she ever was, at least for the next eighteen years.

After they walked her parents out, then checked on Sawyer asleep in the nursery, he turned toward her bedroom—not his.

As they stood in front of her room, he leaned down to kiss her cheek like he was a suitor saying goodnight at her door. "I had a really fun time. I'm glad we called a truce."

Wait. He didn't want to have sex with her? Her pride took a bit of a hit, but she wasn't going to let it show.

"It was a nice evening. Thank you for suggesting it."

"I'll call my attorney tomorrow."

"I don't think there's a rush. It's not a big deal if you don't get to it right away. I'm not going anywhere."

He gave a wry smile. "Not for six weeks, anyway."

They stood in awkward silence.

Please ask me to sleep in your room she chanted in her head as she stared up at him.

He didn't, and instead said, "Well, we should probably get some sleep. Little man is going to be hungry before we know it. I can take the first feeding if you want to take the second."

Sawyer taking a bottle meant Maverick could feed him and let her sleep, which he'd been an amazing sport about. But her pride insisted on reciprocating, so they'd been working in shifts. No more running into each other in the middle of the night.

"That would work better for me to nurse, since the alcohol should be out of my system by then."

He kissed her cheek again, lingering next to her face when he whispered, "Good night, darlin'. Sweet dreams."

She put her hand on his shoulder to catch his lips with hers in a soft, chaste kiss.

"Thank you again for a great night."

His mouth remained inches from hers as he stared into her eyes. "The pleasure was all mine."

CHAPTER THIRTY-SIX

Maverick

He didn't know how to proceed.

It felt like she was giving him signals—something his cock was more than happy about, but they'd just agreed to a truce... wouldn't sex complicate things?

It seemed like every time they had sex they ended up further apart. He didn't want to jeopardize the good feelings between them right now.

But she was so fucking beautiful as she stared up at him with her big hazel eyes.

He decided just to be honest with her.

"I really want to ask you to come to my room, but I don't want to screw up the good thing we seem to have going right now."

"You think if we had sex that would screw it up?"

"It seems to be our pattern."

She suggestively ran her index finger along his chest. "Well, we've never called a truce before."

Maverick ran his hands down her sides and around her backside to grab two handfuls of flesh as he pulled her tight against him. "That's true. We haven't."

Subtly grinding her hips against his while she wrapped her arms around his neck, she murmured, "Just think of all the peace treaty negotiations we could have if we were naked."

He pressed his hard cock against her. "Oh, being naked with you is pretty much all I can think about right now."

"We seem to have an accord then."

He swooped her up in a bridal carry and strode to his room.

"I feel like I'm over a month late doing this."

"Maybe, but things were different on our wedding night. For starters, I hadn't been cleared for intercourse, so I understand why you didn't. Although, we could have done other things."

Why hadn't he done those other things? They should have been intimate on their wedding night. Maybe if he'd made it special, they wouldn't be in the boat they were in.

Hindsight was twenty-twenty.

"I didn't want to push you. I was trying to be respectful"

A seductive smile crossed her lips. "I think we've proven I don't mind being pushed and disrespected a little."

Maverick carefully set her down on the bed.

"Yeah, I know that *now*. Although tonight, I'd like to make love to you, if you don't mind."

****

Olivia

Nope. Uh-uh. They weren't going there.

There would be no love anything between them. It would be too confusing for her.

"How about we make *like*, and you pull my hair as you fuck me hard?"

He considered that for a long moment, until finally he replied, "Yeah, we can do that."

Olivia reached behind her to unzip her dress, letting it fall in a heap at her ankles—suddenly glad she'd foregone the shapewear she'd been considering. She hadn't been sure how the night was going to end, but decided to be prepared, just in case.

Maverick's nostrils flared at the sight of her in her lacy black panties and black thigh highs. The black nursing bra wasn't very sexy, but at least it matched.

"You are so fucking beautiful."

When he looked at her like that, she felt beautiful, which emboldened her to drop to her knees in front of him and look up as she undid his belt and unfastened his pants button.

"Sweetheart," he whispered as he touched her chin. "You don't have to do that."

Olivia froze. What kind of bullshit was that?

She looked him in the eye as she pulled his zipper down. "I enjoy sucking your cock."

That was true—it was a power rush to have him vulnerable and at her mercy.

Tugging his boxer briefs to his knees, his cock bounced as it sprang free. She quickly wrapped her hand around the shaft and drew his length between her lips.

She glanced up to find him with his head thrown back, eyes closed as he wove his fingers in her hair.

"And it enjoys when you suck it."

Maverick let out a low hiss when Olivia took him as deep as she could. She slowly pulled his shaft from her lips, circled the head with her tongue, and drew him back between her lips.

Using her hand, she leisurely jerked him from the base, meeting her mouth in the middle as she moved her head up and down his length.

Gradually, her tempo increased until his grip on her hair tightened at the same time she tasted his precum.

"You need to slow down, darlin'. You're going to make me come."

That only spurred her to keep going.

"Olivia," he warned again.

"I want you to come. I want to taste you."

"Fuuuuck," he groaned.

As if accepting his fate, he used her hair to move her mouth on his cock in the rhythm he wanted. His grunts grew louder and more feral, and she knew he was on the verge of coming. Knowing the vibrations would add to his sensations, she moaned around his shaft.

He bucked his hips as he growled, "Fuck yes!" Seconds later, she was rewarded with his cum flooding her mouth.

Milking his cock until he became too sensitive and begged her to stop, she felt like a warrior princess.

She got up to retrieve a towel from the bathroom and gently cleaned him off, then tossed it toward the hamper.

The towel hadn't even hit the floor before he grabbed her by her ankles and pulled her toward him. Pushing her legs wide, he dragged his tongue along her folds as he murmured, "My turn."

CHAPTER THIRTY-SEVEN

Maverick

"Oh my god," she panted. "How did you get so good at that?"

He chuckled as he wiped his mouth on the sheet, then crawled next to her, pulling her into his arms.

"My mom let me lick the mixer beaters whenever she made a cake. And cakes were our favorite dessert, so she made a lot of them."

"Thank god for the Mitchell boys' sugar cravings. Do you still like cake?"

"I do. But I prefer pussy for dessert."

"I will happily volunteer as tribute; at least until one of us is seeing someone else."

Oh yeah. That was inevitable, given that she was moving out in six weeks.

He didn't dignify that with a response, just kissed her hair and whispered, "Go to sleep."

She easily complied and was soon snoring. Maverick wasn't surprised, considering they were both operating on minimal sleep, and she'd consumed alcohol for the first time since she found out she was pregnant.

It felt nice to have her in his bed again. Holding her without having to pretend he was asleep was a nice bonus.

He dozed off, too, only to be woken a few hours later when Sawyer's cries came through the baby monitor on his nightstand.

Sitting up, he switched it off so as not to wake her, rubbed the sleep from his eyes, and murmured, "I'm coming, little man," before glancing over at Olivia sprawled out, dead to the world.

That made him smile.

Sawyer's cries got louder and starting to come through the walls, so Maverick quickly shuffled to the nursery to retrieve his son before going downstairs to warm up his bottle.

As he sat in the sitting area of the kitchen feeding his little boy in the dark, he realized he needed to cherish his time with him. Things were going to change soon enough, and he wouldn't be with him every night.

Not to mention he was going to grow up. Maverick knew it'd be in the blink of an eye and Sawyer would be starting school.

He made a mental note to talk to her about what schools she wanted to send him to. They could afford private, but the public schools in his neighborhood were top-notch. Nick and Nash had both attended middle and high school there. Hopefully Olivia would be agreeable to using his address, like Patricia had.

That brought him back to thinking about his current wife and all the places he'd gone wrong with her. He'd arrogantly thought once she spent time with him, she wouldn't want to leave. He hadn't factored in her boyfriend actually being real or that she was in love with him.

But he had her for the next six weeks, and he was going to enjoy the hell out of their time together.

**

Sunlight was peeking through the side of the shades when he woke up the next morning. A smile formed on his lips when he remembered falling asleep with her curled against his side. He reached for her, but wasn't surprised to find her side of the bed empty. Glancing at the clock on his nightstand, he sat up with a start when he saw it was nine thirty.

He'd gotten a whole six hours of sleep! That was the most he'd had since November thirtieth, the night before Sawyer was born.

It wasn't until he reached for the monitor like he did every morning, that he realized it was off.

Shit. Did I forget to turn it back on when I came to bed?

No. He distinctly remembered checking on his son one last time before sliding in next to his mother, feeling at peace that his little family was where they were supposed to be.

She must have shut it off when she got up so she wouldn't wake him. He appreciated her courtesy.

After a quick shower and shave, he got dressed and headed downstairs, stopping when he reached the landing and heard her voice.

"Watch mommy." There was a brief pause, and then she said, "See? It's easy! You try."

Sawyer let out his happy shriek, which made her laugh out loud. "That's easy, right?"

He quietly approached the entry to the family room, where he found her laying on the quilt next to his son, manually rolling him over. Then she rolled onto her back and asked, "See how mommy did it?" like she expected an answer.

Sawyer kicked his arms and legs while squealing encouragement to his mother for her efforts.

This. This was what Maverick didn't want to miss out on.

A sense of sadness washed over him. He only had six more weeks before his little family imploded.

And you're not going to waste it moping.

With new resolve to make their remaining time together memorable, he stood up straighter. Yeah, he was unhappy things were going to change, but he was determined to use this time to prove to her they could coparent and get along, and end their marriage on good terms.

He walked into the family room wearing a big smile, asking, "Is your mommy teaching you how to roll over?" as he sat on the other side of the baby.

Sawyer rewarded him immediately with a toothless grin.

Olivia blew her bangs from her forehead. "I'm not doing a very good job. So far he's just laughed at me."

Maverick laid down and did his own demonstration—to the delight of his little boy, and judging by her laughter, his wife.

It was going to be a good day.

Olivia

They spent the next hour playing with their son, then she nursed him while Maverick disappeared into his office with a cup of coffee and a breakfast bar.

At noon Sawyer went down for a nap, so she knocked on the open door to his office. He was sitting at his desk with his glasses on the end of his nose while he stared at the computer screen. She loved that look on him. It made him look distinguished.

"Do you want lunch?"

He flipped the glasses on top of his head, sat back in his chair, and blatantly ran his gaze down her body, then back up to meet her eyes. "I do."

She felt a zing in her lady parts. He was so damn sexy he could turn her on with just a look and two words.

Olivia was both afraid and exhilarated to ask, "What would you like?"

Maverick tossed his glasses on the blotter as he stood and came around his desk to snake an arm around her waist.

"Guess," he whispered, then leaned down to plant his lips on hers.

Wrapping her arms around his neck, she pressed her body against his as their tongues began to tangle. She shamelessly ground her pussy against his hard cock, cursing the fabric that was between them.

When he unbuttoned her jeans and pulled her toward the leather couch in the sitting area of his office, she let out a contented sigh.

She offered an ankle for him to take her jeans off, and with a wink, he obliged, then dropped between her thighs.

"Why darlin'," he said with a grin as he ran a finger down her seam. "It appears you're already wet for me."

Olivia closed her eyes and shamelessly spread her knees wider when she felt his hot breath on her center. "Huh, I wonder how that happened."

Planting kisses on the inside of her thigh, he asked, "I wonder if you taste as good as you look?"

She dug her fingers into his short hair to pull him closer.

He seemed intent on going slow and teasing her until she whispered a reminder, "Juanita should be here soon."

"Dammit. I better eat fast, then, so I can fuck you for dessert."

He wasted no time and buried his face in her pussy; licking and sucking as he pressed two fingers inside her. With his other hand, he pulled the hood on her clit back and flicked his tongue rapidly along her exposed nub.

Lifting her back off the couch, she let out a long moan as she felt her body temperature start to rise.

"Just like that, Mav. Oh god, just like that."

He responded by increasing the tempo of his fingers to match his tongue, and she felt her climax start to roll over her body.

"Don't stop," she implored. "Please don't stop."

She heard him take a deep breath through his nose before he doubled his efforts.

Her entire being zinged with the electricity of her impending orgasm as he took her higher and higher. Then with a long moan, her body spasmed as she floated back down.

He quickly dispatched his own jeans and boxer-briefs and slid between her thighs as he put his arms on either side of her body.

Holding her shoulders, he slid inside her with one thrust.

"Fuuuuck," he growled as he pistoned his hips, plunging in and out.

She clung to his broad back and moaned her agreement. She loved the masculine, woodsy scent of his skin as he drove into her pussy, hitting just the right spot so another orgasm began to build in her belly.

His mastery of her body had her coming again at the same time he exploded inside her with a feral grunt. Just the sound of him coming could probably make her orgasm—it was so damn sexy.

Like everything else about him.

They'd just gotten dressed when his phone chimed the alert for the camera at the door.

He grinned at her with a wink. "Perfect timing."

CHAPTER THIRTY-EIGHT

Olivia

It was ten o'clock at night when she finished feeding and changing Sawyer. She rocked him in the rocking chair in the corner by the book shelf that now overflowed with books.

As word of Maverick's new son had spread to his family and colleagues, presents started pouring in. Many followed the new trend that she loved of including a book in lieu of a card. It was such a cozy area—she could picture herself reading to him on the rug when he got older. Or Sawyer studying books for hours by himself, like she used to when she was a child.

It made her sad when she realized she wouldn't be here when he got older.

It's okay, he has a great room at my place with plenty of books.

Granted, the difference between her house and Maverick's was like a Hilton hotel versus a Ritz-Carlton. While Hiltons were perfectly comfortable, they were nothing like a stay at the Ritz.

She gently laid him in his crib and watched him sleep for a few minutes.

"Goodnight little one," she said softly before clicking the light off and going into her room to change into the sexy pajama set Rose had sent her as a gift for the bridal shower she refused to have.

After brushing her hair and teeth, she slipped her robe on and headed down the hall. Halfway to Maverick's room, it hit her.

Was she being presumptuous? They'd never discussed their sleeping arrangements. Last night might have been a one-off. Yeah, they'd called a truce, but that didn't necessarily mean he wanted her in his bed every night. He hadn't extended the invitation.

The closer she got to his room, the more she doubted what she was doing.

When she opened the door and found his room dark, with soft snoring sounds coming from his bed, she realized the idea had been solely one-sided on her part.

Olivia quickly backed out and closed the door. She could tell her cheeks were red from embarrassment. God, she was glad he was asleep. How humiliating would *that* have been?

Of course, he would have been polite, probably even welcoming. But they were obviously on different pages about what this truce meant.

Still, their time together since calling the truce had been wonderful, so she was going to get up tomorrow expecting more of the same. After all, the clock was ticking on their arrangement, and she was going to enjoy it while it lasted.

****

Maverick

He'd been sitting in bed doing some work on his tablet while he waited for Olivia to finish nursing Sawyer. Occasionally, he'd glance up and watch her on the baby monitor with his son, and his heart would skip a beat.

My little family.

Once she shut the nursery lights off, he waited for her to walk through the bedroom door.

But she never came.

He was disappointed. Although they hadn't talked about it, he thought for sure after their last twenty-four hours together, she would be moving back into the owner's suite.

That's what he got for assuming.

With a sigh, he shut the lights out and promptly fell asleep, knowing he needed to be up in a few hours to feed Sawyer.

Ever since their son started taking a bottle, he and Olivia had fallen into a routine where she put the baby down for the night while Maverick went to bed so he could get up for the middle of the night shift. She would get up for the next feeding, then would usually lay back down for a few more hours before they both got up and started their day.

Maverick woke up earlier than he had since bringing Sawyer home from the hospital, and went down to the kitchen to start breakfast.

He had a steady rhythm going at the stove when he heard her say, "Something smells good."

He turned to find her sitting down at the kitchen island with her hair still sticking up, wrapped in a white fuzzy robe.

"Good morning. I hope you're hungry."

"Starving. Somehow, I managed to burn a lot of calories yesterday."

She was grinning when he looked over at her.

He flipped a pancake, then replied, "What a coincidence; I did too. I wonder how that happened."

"Oh, I remember exactly how it happened."

So did he. Every little noise she made, every quiver of her thighs, every arch of her back... they were etched in his memory.

He glanced at her as he added the pancake from the pan to a stack already on a plate, then slid it in front of her. "Oh yeah? Anything worth repeating?"

"Gosh, I hope so," she said as she swiped her knife in the tub of butter he'd already set on the counter, along with the syrup. "Otherwise, the next six weeks will be very disappointing."

He stared at her pretty face as he murmured, "We wouldn't want that."

Olivia maintained eye contact when she replied, "No, we wouldn't."

Maverick was the first to look away. He picked up the bowl of batter and poured more into the frying pan. A sizzling noise escaped the second it hit the skillet.

"The sun's supposed to be out today. Do you want to go do something fun, then grab some lunch at Flannigan's?"

She studied him as she chewed a bite of food. "What do you consider fun?"

"It's funny, because I was going to ask you the same thing. What sounds like a fun day to you?"

"Depends on the time of year, I guess. Obviously, in the summer, anything on the water makes me happy."

"What about now?"

"Honestly? I don't know."

"Okay, let's say a year ago, before you got pregnant, what would the ideal winter day have looked like?

She took another bite, chewing slowly as she thought. Finally, she said, "I've spent the last twelve years working my tail off. An ideal day would have been one where I could sleep in, do some laundry, and binge watch my favorite Netflix show while eating junk food that I'd had delivered."

"We can do that."

Olivia laughed as she shook her head. "I feel like that's all I've done for the last two months. Well, minus eating the delivered junk food. Juanita has provided me with infinitely better choices."

"So... what sounds fun?"

"I haven't been to the museum in a while. That might be interesting."

He nodded his agreement. "Let finish breakfast, then get ready."

****

Olivia

The museum turned out to be good time. They only toured the Ancient Greece, Rome and Byzantine Empire exhibit, but they spent a few hours there.

Maverick carried Sawyer against his chest in the baby sling, and she noticed more than one mom chaperoning a group of school kids swoon at the sight of the silver fox and infant son.

Olivia wasn't jealous.

Not at all.

That *wasn't* why she made sure to slip her hand into his with a smile or lean her head against him when he'd put his arm around her shoulder as they studied a piece.

The three of them were greeted warmly when they walked into Flannigan's mid-afternoon for lunch. All the waitresses fawned over their happy boy as he smiled brightly from his stroller, and even Dan came around the bar and asked if he could hold him.

Maverick cocked his head and said, "Sure, man. I never would have pegged you for the kid type."

"Are you kidding? I'm aching to have 'em. I just need to find the right woman. But I'm not settling, so... here I am."

"You'll find her," Olivia proclaimed with authority.

Maverick put his hand on hers and smiled. "You just have to be patient."

When he looked at her like that, it made it hard to breathe.

This is ending in six weeks. Knock that shit off.

She waited until Dan walked away with Sawyer to subtly pull her hand away. Smiling sweetly, she asked, "Did you get a hold of your attorney today?"

He jerked his head back with a frown. "You told me there wasn't a rush."

"Oh, there's not, I was just wondering."

And trying to keep some perspective.

A noticeable chill hovered between them, and she instantly regretted bringing it up.

"I'm sorry. I didn't mean to kill the good vibe between us."

"It's fine," he replied dismissively without looking at her.

"I don't feel like it is." Olivia grabbed his hand, refusing to let go or look away until he acknowledged her. When he did, she stared into his eyes while she squeezed his hand. "I really am sorry. It was a completely inappropriate time to bring that up. Please forgive me."

He gave her a weak smile but leaned over and kissed her cheek. "Apology accepted."

Her mom ears perked up at the sound of her son's cry from across the bar. Maverick heard it, too, and turned around to locate where it was coming from.

Dan transferred Sawyer to a shoulder hold and started to pat his back. She was impressed with the bartender's paternal instincts.

The fix was only temporary, however, because a few minutes later Sawyer started crying again, and Dan made a beeline back to their table and transferred the crying infant into her waiting arms, where he immediately quieted.

"He's getting tired," she offered apologetically when she noticed Dan seemed to take the baby's crying in his arms personally.

Maverick appeared to pick up on that, too, because he offered, "And he might need to be changed."

The younger man observed the now quiet infant nestled against her chest and whispered wistfully, "He's beautiful. Congratulations. You two are so lucky."

She kissed the dark, downy hair on her son's head. "We are."

Fucking Maverick's eyes shone as he stared at the two of them and murmured his agreement. "So lucky."

Six weeks.

Yet, she couldn't decide if she was looking forward to March tenth, or dreading it.

CHAPTER THIRTY-NINE

Maverick

Their truce had been going marvelously over the last two weeks, and during that time they'd ventured out as a family three times, had quickies in his office, on the kitchen counter, the bathroom counter, the washing machine, and the floor of the family room. And last Saturday night they'd managed to go out to dinner alone again, with Sawyer staying at her parents' house—and her in his bed.

"Good morning," he said when he noticed her eyes open.

"Good morning," she said with a soft laugh. "I forgot where I was for a second."

He wanted to suggest she move back into his room, forever. But that seemed to go against the unspoken terms of their truce.

"You okay waking up here?"

"Yeah, it was nice. Probably shouldn't make a habit of it, though."

God forbid.

"I liked waking up next to you."

"You just liked sleeping all night," she teased.

He rolled on top of her and boxed her in between his arms. "If I recall correctly, we didn't do a lot of sleeping."

She smiled as she tugged the sheet above her mouth. "No we did not. But you've brushed your teeth and I haven't, so you need to let me up."

"I don't care."

"I do. Besides, I have to pee."

He reluctantly rolled back onto his side of the bed while she disappeared into the bathroom.

"Tomorrow's Valentine's Day," he called from the bed when he heard the water shut off.

Olivia peeked around the corner as she wiped her face with a hand towel. "So?"

"Do you want to go to dinner or something?"

She came back into the room and sat down on the bed. "I think my mom and dad's 'grandparenting-is-fun' meter is going to be pegged after Sawyer's sleepover last night."

"We'll bring him with us."

She shot him a look. "A crying baby while people are out enjoying what's supposed to be the most romantic night of the year? No thank you. I'm not going to be *that* mom. Besides, it's not like we're a real couple and need to celebrate."

"I'm going to have to call bullshit. We're a real couple for the next month."

"You know what I mean."

Yeah, he did; it didn't mean he had to like it.

"We have to do something."

"Fine, but no gifts! Why don't I make dinner and we can watch a movie?"

"You can cook?"

"Believe it or not, I can. I just haven't in a long time— cooking for myself doesn't excite me that much."

Maverick was curious to see this domestic side of her. "Okay, let's do that, then."

"It's a date." She quickly added, "But not really."

He didn't respond, but inside he was screaming, *It* is *a date, dammit.*

"I need to go into the office today. Are you okay to get Sawyer alone?"

"Wait. *The office?* You have an office?"

"Complete with a staff and everything."

"Have you gone in since I've been here?"

"I stopped in to let my assistant, Pam, know I was going to be working from home. She sends me everything I need to work on and handles the rest herself."

"How did I not know you have an office?"

"I own the building the office is in, too. Actually, I have several office buildings.

"How's brag camp going?"

That made him laugh out loud. "I'm not bragging, I'm just telling you since you seemed upset you didn't know I had an office."

"I was just teasing. Thank you for telling me, although it's completely unnecessary. It's none of my business."

"Mmm, it kind of is. If I died of a heart attack, half my estate would go to you. Actually, more than half. A half and a third of the other half that's Sawyer's."

"Wouldn't it just go to Nick and Nash?"

He furrowed his brow. "No. I have three sons, and a wife."

"But we barely got married..."

"I redrafted my will the day I found out Sawyer was mine. Then again when you signed the prenup."

"Oh."

"So, back to my original question. Are you okay to get Sawyer by yourself?"

"Of course I am. And if I wasn't, I probably should start practicing since I'm going to be doing it alone here in a month. I just need the car seat."

He shook his head. "I got one for your car, too. It's already installed."

She looked at him dumbfounded. "You did that?"

"Of course. It made sense to have one in each car. The nice thing is, the base is the same, so the seat and stroller are interchangeable."

"Oh, wow. That is nice. Thank you."

That was one of many things he loved about her. She always made sure to express her gratitude whenever anyone did something nice for her.

"Of course."

****

Olivia

She almost dropped her coffee mug when Maverick walked into the kitchen wearing a suit and tie.

The man was panty-melting gorgeous in business attire.

"Wow. You look great."

"I'm meeting with a group who wants me to invest in their coffee business." He winked, "I have to look the part of Mr. Potter."

That made her smile as she approached him to straighten the knot on his tie. "No, you're definitely George Bailey."

With a grin, he said, "I wasn't sure if you'd get the *It's a Wonderful Life* reference. And I'm no George Bailey."

"I got it, and I beg to differ. You're George—just ask Frank Symanski. And I'll bet there's a dozen other people exactly like Frank who you've helped."

She brushed his shoulders with the backs of her fingertips, then double tapped his chest. "You're a good man, Pete Mitchell. Sawyer won the dad lottery when..." Olivia glanced down. "Well, I tricked you into getting me pregnant."

He lifted her chin with his knuckle. "I'm thankful you did. I love—" he paused briefly, then continued, "that little boy more than I knew was possible. My only regret is that I didn't know you were pregnant. I would have been your three a.m. cravings connection. And I would have put your furniture together, and not made you have Evan do it."

"No, you wouldn't have. You would have made me move in here sooner."

He chuckled unapologetically. "Yeah, that's true. But it would have been easier to handle your cravings that way."

"Oh my god. I was either hungry or horny. My poor vibrator got a workout."

"Why didn't Casey help with that? With everything, really?"

She'd let that lie marinate for so long, there was no way she could get out of it now.

"Oh, he did, when he could. I mean, more the food part than anything. Me being pregnant with someone else's baby made the sex part weird, so we decided we'd wait when it came to that."

She thought that flowed with the other lies she'd spewed.

Maverick eyed her suspiciously. "And you aren't in contact with him now?"

She swallowed hard.

I haven't talked to him in over two years and don't care if I ever do again.

"No. I'm waiting until our divorce is final. I wouldn't do that to you."

His scowl suggested he was skeptical of her answer, but he let the matter drop.

With a kiss to her forehead, he said, "I'll be home before five. Drive carefully and thank your parents for me."

"I will. Have fun playing Mr. Potter, George."

CHAPTER FORTY

Maverick

The next day, he went into the office again to get a few things done before D-Day. That was what he'd come to think of March tenth, the day she went back to work. He had no idea if she planned on moving out the weekend before. That would really suck.

The very idea of her leaving made him sick to his stomach, but he'd given her his word he'd file for divorce, so he wasn't going to fight her about it.

There were times when he could swear she felt the same way about him, then she'd bring up moving out like she couldn't wait to be free of him.

It was Valentine's Day, and he was in a quandary.

When he bought her engagement and wedding rings, he'd bought earrings, too, intending to give them to her on their one-year anniversary.

Since there wasn't going to be an anniversary, he still wanted her to have them—even if it was just to pawn them with her rings.

On one hand, she was still his wife and the mother of his child, so giving her a Valentine's present was completely justifiable. On the other, she'd said no gifts.

He decided they'd be from Sawyer. Yeah, it was a loophole, but so what. He also sent her two dozen roses from her son.

Two hours later, his phone rang. He looked down to see her name on his screen and smiled.

"Hi there."

"Don't 'hi there' me, Pete Mitchell. What did I say about no gifts?"

"I didn't get you a gift."

"Oh, so Sawyer called up the florist, used his credit card, and had two dozen red roses delivered to me?"

"Well, he asked me to, so I helped him out."

She sighed. "Dammit, Maverick. They're so beautiful, and they smell so good, and now I'm going to have to get the baby dressed and go out and buy you something from him. And to top it off, I have no idea what to get you. You have every tool known to man, more clothes than any guy I've ever met, and I can't afford to buy you a new car."

That made him laugh.

"I don't know, I think I lost a few tools last month, somehow."

"I didn't lose any of your tools, just may have rearranged them when I was looking for the hammer."

"I thought it was a screwdriver..."

"Whatever."

"And, actually, you can afford whatever you want—you're still my wife."

"Like I'd spend your money. And that's not even the point!"

"Look," he said calmly. "You don't need to *buy* me anything. You're making me dinner—that's my present."

"It's not the same."

"Are you kidding? It's better. You're putting effort into this meal. I just made a phone call. If anything, your present is way more thoughtful."

"You still shouldn't have gotten me anything." Her pout came through the phone, and he couldn't help but smile as he pictured her with her arms folded across her chest with a scowl on her face.

"Like I said, I didn't."

"Then I guess I don't need to worry about thanking you properly."

His face fell at that, and he cried, "Aw, no fair."

"Sorry, I don't make the rules."

He wasn't sure that was true. It sure seemed like she did.

****

Olivia

After preparing her mother's green bean casserole recipe and popping it in the oven, she marinated the New York strips, peeled the potatoes and put them on the stove to boil, and prepped the salad. She even had handmade rolls ready to bake. All she had left to do was mash the potatoes, put the meat on the grill, and marinate the mushrooms to top the steaks.

After proudly surveying her work, she turned to Sawyer, who'd been keeping her company from his car seat on the kitchen island. "Your mommy would've made an awesome chef. Your daddy better be impressed."

"If it tastes as good as it smells, you have nothing to worry about," came his deep voice from the laundry room doorway.

She let out a squeak as she jumped.

"Oh my god, you scared me! You can't sneak up on people like that!"

His brows knitted, and he glanced behind him. "I came in through the garage…"

"Well, you need a noisier garage door, then!"

He chuckled as walked in and planted a kiss on her forehead, then greeted their son with a "Hello!" and an animated smile that their happy boy quickly returned.

Maverick set the leather messenger bag he used to carry his laptop and other work documents on the ground and pulled Sawyer from the seat.

"How's my little guy today? Did you help your mama cook dinner?"

Sawyer intently watched Maverick's mouth move, then tried to grab his nose, but wasn't quite coordinated enough yet. Maverick grabbed the baby's hand and pretended to eat it, to the child's delight.

The sound of baby laughter filled the room, and Olivia paused to appreciate it. At the same time, a sense of sadness washed over her. Would she ever have this again? With someone who loved her, not just liked her a lot because they shared a son?

Maverick

"What can I do to help?" he asked as he watched her scurry around the kitchen, careful to stay out of her way.

"Nothing. This is *your* present, remember?"

That made him want to wrap his arms around her and tell her she was silly, that he didn't need a present. But the way she bustled around, it was obvious she was a woman on a mission, and asking her to pause would be an unwelcome intrusion.

He decided to take another tack instead.

"Do you want me to grill the steaks?"

She paused mid-flitter and looked at him. "Are you asking because you think only men can work a grill or to be helpful?"

That answer was obvious.

"To be helpful, of course. You deliver babies for a living, I have no doubt you can operate a grill. Girl power!"

She pressed her lips together like she was trying to fight her smile. "I like mine medium."

It was frickin' freezing out, and for a second he wondered if she'd tricked him, then he remembered he was the one who offered in the first place.

He looked at his watch and dashed back inside to wait until he needed to flip the steaks.

"Brrrr!" he said as he stamped his feet on the mat.

"I thought we'd eat in the dining room, if that's okay."

"Of course. This is your house, too, Olivia. You don't need my permission to do anything."

The unspoken *for another month* hung in the air but neither voiced it.

When he came back inside with the New York strips, he took them directly into the dining room where the table was set, including the side dishes.

Next to his plate sat a small package wrapped in red and pink paper.

"What's this?" he asked as he sat down.

"Just something from Sawyer."

"Can I open it now?"

"No, wait until after dinner."

Maverick pulled the earrings from his pocket. Pam had been wrapping her husband's present at the office and had some of the purple, red, and pink hearts paper left over—enough to wrap the small box, anyway.

He set the package next to her place setting. "Sawyer got you something, too."

She shot him the dirty look he'd been expecting.

"Dammit, Maverick."

"I'm sorry, I don't make the rules, Hallmark does. And, apparently a new mother getting a Valentine's present from her baby is like a cardinal rule, so there's no way I was going to let my son violate that."

"You're not funny."

"Come on, I'm kind of funny."

"Not even the littlest bit."

He'd come to know when she was trying to act mad, but really wasn't, so he felt confident cockily replying, "You can admit it," as he put the medium cut of meat on her plate.

"You're impossible, is what you are."

"Impossibly loveable."

He knew he was pushing the envelope with that remark.

She scooped mashed potatoes onto her plate and handed him the bowl.

"You have your moments."

Victory!

He was going to quit while he was ahead.

They finished preparing their plates and started to eat.

"Darlin', this is delicious. You outdid yourself."

"Thank you."

The conversation that flowed was easy, although somewhat innocuous. She told him about Sawyer's antics that afternoon, he bitched about the traffic coming home.

The domesticity of their dinner added to the perfection.

"Should we open presents before dessert?" he asked.

The package that sat next to his plate had been taunting him all through their meal, and he couldn't wait anymore. He was dying to know what it was.

"Sure..."

"I'll go first!"

A small smile formed on her lips. "Don't get too excited," she told him, but he was already ripping into the paper. He felt like a kid at Christmas.

Maverick burst out laughing when he saw what it was. One of his missing tape measures.

"I was wondering what happened to this."

"I sort of hid of it."

"You don't say..."

She shrugged unapologetically.

"Okay, you next," he encouraged.

Giving him the side-eye, she unwrapped her gift much more slowly than he had. She paused when she saw the jeweler's name imprinted on the top of the lid, then lifted the top like a snake might jump out at her.

A small gasp escaped her lips when she saw the earrings, then she looked up at him with a scowl.

"Goddammit, Pete. Why? *Why*?! We had a deal. I let the flowers slide, but this... this is too much."

He noticed that lately she only called him Pete when she was upset with him.

"Okay. Hold on. I got these when I bought your engagement and wedding rings, so this was planned months ago, before you made the 'no gifts' rule."

He didn't mention they were supposed to be a first-year anniversary gift before adding, "Why don't you try them on before you get too mad at me."

She did just that, then looked in the mirror on the wall and stomped her foot like a petulant child. .

"Maaaan, they're beautiful." Then she begrudgingly added, "Thank you."

He chuckled, "You're welcome."

"Are you ready for dessert?"

He was, but probably not the kind she was referring to.

"Yeah, let me help," he answered, picking up their finished plates to follow her into the kitchen.

Setting the dishes on the counter next to the sink, he grabbed her around the waist and lifted her onto the granite island.

"I told you that your pussy is my favorite dessert," he said as he tugged on her yoga pants.

She didn't argue, just leaned back on her elbows and lifted her butt to help him take her leggings and panties off.

He spread her legs wide and sat down on the bar stool in front of her, grinning like a fat cat with a bowl of cream.

"You look downright delectable, sweetheart."

He wasted no time and dove head-first between her thighs. His tongue leisurely explored her folds as she mewled her appreciation of his performance. When he circled her clit and pressed a finger inside, she arched off the stone with a soft moan, then slid her hands across the smooth surface, as if seeking purchase when he rapidly flicked his tongue back and forth while adding a second finger.

"Oh my god!"

Her body went taut, and he knew she was close, so he replaced his tongue with his other hand in order to polish her pearl with more pressure.

"Come for me, Olivia. I want to taste my delicious wife."

"Maverick! Yes! Oh god, just like that!"

He doubled down his efforts, and she chanted, "Yes! Yes! Yes!" until she lurched off the countertop as her body spasmed from head to toe and she cried out, "Fuuuuuck!'

Maverick looked up with a satisfied smile. Making his wife come was his new favorite pastime.

"You are so good at that," she panted.

"Sweetheart, you taste so fucking good, I could eat you every day, twice a day, and want more."

"I think I would self-combust from orgasm-overload."

"No such thing, darlin'."

She sat up and glanced around the room.

"I saw something in a porno once that I've always wanted to try."

His ears perked up. "You have my attention."

****

Olivia

"The island might be too high, although..." she looked at where his waist hit the counter. "You are pretty tall. Let's try it. If it doesn't work, we'll move to the dining room table."

"Try what? Use your words, woman!"

She spun around and put her back to him, then laid down, so her head was off the counter.

"I'd rather show you."

He stared at her, not moving, then finally mumbled, "That's fucking hot," as he reached for his belt.

CHAPTER FORTY-ONE

Olivia

After their tryst in the kitchen Maverick helped her clean up from dinner, then slipped away to his home office to get some work done while she nursed Sawyer and prepared him for bed.

As she sat in the rocking chair in the nursery, she thought about her and Maverick's time together since calling a truce. It had been wonderful, but every day it seemed to hurt a little more. Being in love with a man who treated her well and was amazing in bed sucked when the man in question didn't love her back. His kindness felt almost cruel at times.

How was any another man going to be able to measure up to him?

Thanks for ruining all men for me, Pete.

Olivia shook her head. No! She'd find someone someday. She had to, right? She was entitled to be with a man who loved her.

"Mommy's going to get a new husband," she told Sawyer as she stared down at him at her breast. "And he'll treat us just as great as your daddy."

Even as she said the words, she knew they were a lie. No man—even if he did love her and Sawyer—would care for them like Maverick did.

In her heart, she knew Maverick would let her stay if she wanted. They were perfectly happy and got along well, but she knew the longer she was there, the more it was going to hurt in the end.

"I deserve the fairytale."

****

Maverick

He couldn't help but feel slighted as he sat in his office listening to the baby monitor.

She deserves the fairytale?

What the fuck else did he have to do to prove how much he cared about her and Sawyer?

That's when he realized it didn't matter what he did, because she was in love with someone else. Sure, she was letting him scratch her sexual itch, but that's all it had been. That was obvious when she didn't want to sleep in his bed with him.

He even understood her inability to fall in love with him. If she was in love with another man, it wasn't going to happen. He almost felt sorry for the next woman he dated. There's no way she'd be able to measure up to Olivia—kind of like Maverick couldn't measure up to Casey.

Their marriage was going to end. The sooner he accepted that, the better off he'd be. This truce might have been a bad idea, at least for his heart. Although his tools were better off for it.

He stayed in his office another hour just to make sure she was asleep when he walked past her room. He wasn't sure what he would do if they passed each other in the hall.

The next morning he decided it would be better if he spent more time in the office and away from her.

"Back at it again?" she asked with a smile when he walked into the kitchen wearing a suit.

"Yesterday I realized I'm more behind than I thought."

"Just so you know, I'm able to use the hospital daycare, so if you aren't able to take care of him when—"

He cut her off. "I'll take him to the office with me. Pam squealed when she saw me ordering a playpen and toys yesterday. She can't wait to have a baby in the office."

"She sounds lovely. I'd like to meet her sometime."

"Of course. Sawyer is going to be spoiled rotten; you have nothing to worry about."

"I'm not worried. Well—the 'rotten' part worries me a little, but I know you'd never let anything bad happen to him."

"Never."

She scrutinized him for a beat, then said softly, "I know."

Maverick liked that she trusted him. Too bad she couldn't love him.

The sounds of Sawyer waking up came through the monitor, and she stood from the bar stool she'd been sitting on while she drank her coffee.

"Give him a kiss for me," he said as he reluctantly walked toward the door. It was killing him not to be there when his son got out of bed.

"I will." She paused and turned back to ask, "How late are you going to be today?"

He wanted to say he'd be home by noon, but knew he needed to avoid her as much as possible.

"I should be home by dinner. Juanita said she was bringing tamales."

"She loves you."

At least somebody does.

"I'm a loveable guy."

She gave him a wistful smile, but didn't say anything other than, "See you tonight."

"Don't forget to give my boy a kiss."

"I won't."

****

Olivia

Maverick went into the office every day that week, even on Saturday, and on Sunday he holed up in his office with Sawyer while he urged her to 'go out and have fun.'

Things had definitely changed between them. While their truce seemed to still be in effect and he was as kind and gracious as ever, the kisses when he got home were now reserved only for Sawyer. And there hadn't even been a hint that he wanted her sexually anymore. Olivia had no idea why.

Maybe he had a girlfriend at the office?

That seemed unlikely. The first night she met him he'd told her he was as faithful as they came. She believed it then, and she believed it now. Besides, he wouldn't risk nullifying the prenup when they were so close to getting divorced, anyway.

Maybe she should have been more gracious when she first unwrapped the diamond earrings from 'Sawyer' instead of giving Maverick the stink eye. But she had made sure to thank him properly, even though she'd threatened otherwise when they'd talked on the phone.

And if he'd thought she was rude, which, okay, she had been, it had been more for show than anything. But even if he didn't know it'd been for show—which she was pretty sure he did—it didn't seem like his style to hold a grudge over something like that. Not to mention, she'd been sure to wear them every day so he knew she loved them.

That was the only reason she could come up with.

Frankly, she missed him. Not just the sex, although that had been amazing, but their conversations. She had hoped when she moved out they'd still have them, but considering they'd gotten a lot more superficial and they were still living under the same roof, she wasn't optimistic.

She needed to shake things up.

CHAPTER FORTY-TWO

Maverick

They hadn't had sex in almost a week, and he was having a hard time even sitting at the kitchen island without getting stiff, thinking about her hanging her head upside down off the granite and pulling his cock deep into her throat.

The woman was a goddess. He knew that the first night he met her. Living with her these last few months only solidified that. He had no idea how he was supposed to change his feelings for her, but he knew he needed to try. Not having sex seemed like the best place to start. If they kept screwing he'd never get her out of his system. He wasn't stupid.

Or maybe he was.

Because he almost believed her when she showed up at three a.m. feigning she thought it was her turn to feed Sawyer—even though they'd been on this schedule for a few weeks now.

But the lacy black negligee she had on when he met her in the hall had him suspicious. He'd never seen it before. He would definitely have remembered the way it made his cock move.

****

Olivia

She heard Sawyer start to cry in the middle of the night and swung her legs off the bed, then checked the mirror one last time for any price tags she might have missed.

It was hard to say, "Oh, this old thing?" when there was proof it was anything but.

Olivia had decided to pull out the sexy negligee Rose had made her buy for her wedding night. The one she'd never used.

"There's no time like the present," she'd murmured when she put it on. Then she laid down and fell asleep. The past few weeks, she'd been able to shut off listening for Sawyer's cry at three a.m., since that was when Maverick got up with him. Not tonight. Tonight she'd decided to get up, too.

She waited to come out of her room until she heard his bedroom door open, then she walked out and ran into him in the hall—as planned.

And the look he gave her when he saw what she was wearing was also according to plan.

So far, so good.

"What are you doing up?" he asked, his voice raspy with sleep.

"I thought it was my turn to feed him?"

He cocked his head with an amused smile.

"No, I've been taking the middle of the night shift for a while now."

"Oh, well, since I'm up, I'll nurse him. You can go back to bed."

He hesitated, exactly like she thought he would.

Then he said, "Okay, I'll get up with him at six."

And turned around.

What. The. Hell?

**

He was up and gone when she woke up the next morning. The note on the counter told her Sawyer had been fed and changed, and he'd be home for dinner.

Olivia decided she'd try one more time. She went to her room around four to do her hair and makeup and put on clean clothes—free of baby vomit.

She cringed when she caught a glimpse of herself before jumping in the shower. No wonder he wasn't attracted to her anymore. When did she turn into a frump?

Although she hadn't been frumpy last night. Far from it.

When he walked through the door, she looked up from where she was nursing Sawyer in the little nook in the kitchen. He looked tired as he loosened his red and blue striped tie.

"Hi. Everything go okay?"

"As expected."

"I'm sorry about the crossed wires last night. I blame it on my lack of sleep. I hope I didn't screw your schedule up too badly."

"It was fine. I actually had a chance to work out."

That made her jerk her head up.

"You worked out? With who?"

It came out way more accusatory than she'd intended.

The corner of his mouth turned up.

"No one. I ran on the treadmill before I left for the office."

"Oh."

Of course, he'd meant actually working out, not the euphemism they'd referred to as 'working out'.

"Something smells good," he observed.

"I put one of Juanita's lasagnas in the oven. It should be ready soon."

"Let me go get changed, then I'll take care of getting him a new diaper."

He returned ten minutes later dressed in a pair of jeans and a Navy sweatshirt, and took Sawyer from her. As usual, he was beaming when he started his nightly conversation with his son.

"How's my little man, today? Were you a good boy for your mom?"

"He's getting closer to rolling over. I bet any day now."

So, maybe you should stay home this week.

"Don't do it without me, okay, buddy?"

Their son cooed like he was agreeing to what his father just asked.

She got up and pulled the lasagna from the oven and set it on the stove to cool before she cut it.

"Can I ask you a question?" she asked as she set the oven mitts on the counter.

"Shoot."

"What happened to our truce?"

"What do you mean? We've been getting along."

"Sure, but we used to... talk more, and stuff."

Like, you know... have sex? Cuddle? Kiss?

He didn't pick up her cues.

"I'm sorry. I know we did. I've just been busy with work, and I've been trying to give you time with Sawyer before you go back to work. Which reminds me. Do you know what day you're planning on moving out? I want to be sure to be off that day so I can help you."

Jesus, why don't you just show me the door now?

"I don't have that much. Just my clothes and I'll take some of Sawyer's, too."

"Of course. When you know your work schedule we'll be able to plan our schedule for him."

Part of her had been secretly hoping he'd realize he didn't want her to leave, and would find a way to insist that she stay. Apparently, he couldn't wait to get rid of her.

Which must have been what made her blurt out, "I'm thinking about going back to work next week. Rose really needs me—she's swamped."

That was *kinda* true. Rose was swamped, but no more than normal. The temporary doctor they'd hired to fill in for Olivia was working out great. So great, the two had talked about offering her a partnership in the practice.

He put Sawyer in the bouncy seat and walked slowly to the cupboards with the plates in it.

"Next week? Are you sure you're ready? Can't you just go back a few days a week to start?"

She could. Especially if they asked Dr. Lane to join their business.

"I don't think so."

"Hmm. Okay, well, we'll make it work, then."

They'll make it work.

Not, "don't go," or "Please stay."

No, they'd fucking make it work.

CHAPTER FORTY-THREE

Olivia

"I think that's everything," Maverick said when he brought the last suitcase from the Cullinan inside her house.

He looked around the house that hadn't been lived in for three months.

"Your place is nice. It suits you. I can see why you didn't want to leave it."

I did want to, but you didn't want me, so here I am.

"Thank you. I think it's going to feel like living in squalor after living at your house all this time."

"Nah. It's beautiful. You'll feel right at home in no time. Can I see Sawyer's nursery?"

Now, *that* she was proud of. The baby animals theme was adorable, if she did say so herself. She'd used greens and yellows because she'd refused to tell anyone the sex of the baby before he was born. She'd wanted people to focus on that mystery rather than who the father of her child was.

"Wow," he said when he walked in. His smile seemed sad when he looked at her. Sawyer was asleep in the sling attached to her front, and he reached to gently stroke his son's hair. "He's going to be happy here."

"I hope so. My place doesn't compare to yours."

"It's not a contest, Olivia. He'll be loved and cared for no matter where he is. And you'll be getting two million dollars soon, so if you want to move, you can."

"I almost forgot about that. I'm still not sure how I feel about accepting it."

"It's not negotiable. And, we haven't talked about spousal maintenance and child support, yet."

"I make a nice living, Mav. I don't need spousal support, other than maybe a little moral support every now and then." That made him genuinely smile, and she continued, "And since he'll be with you probably more than he'll be with me, I don't think child support is in order."

"Spousal support and child support were part of the contract, Olivia."

And that's another thing. He never called her *sweetheart* or *darlin'* anymore. Everything was her name.

"Well, since we're altering the custody terms, I think we can alter that, too."

"I just want you to have choices. If you decide you're not ready to go back full-time, I want you to feel like you can without worrying financially."

She felt her shoulders droop. "That's really kind of you. Thank you. Maybe we can talk about that if the need arises."

"I'd rather just have it in the divorce decree so you know you're guaranteed the money. You don't *have* to spend it. You can put it in an account for Sawyer, or, hell, give it to charity, but I want you to feel secure."

Why did he have to be such a good guy? Why couldn't he be the asshole who'd shown up at her hospital room?

Olivia sighed at the thought because he hadn't even really been an asshole then, just more insistent about how things were going to go.

She missed bossy Maverick. Accommodating Maverick was annoying her.

Except when he didn't accommodate her.

Yes, she knew what that made her sound like.

"Would you like to stay for dinner? I don't really have anything, but we could have something delivered."

He stared at her for a beat before shaking his head. "I better not."

"Oh, okay."

She walked him to do the door,

"What time do you want me to pick him up tomorrow?"

"Is nine too early?"

"No, but don't worry about me. Just tell me your schedule and we'll make it work."

We'll make it work. Her new least fucking favorite words.

**

Olivia closed the door behind him and hadn't finished turning the lock when the first tear started to fall. She'd been so focused on keeping up the façade that she wasn't sad about leaving, the minute she let her guard down she was a blubbering mess.

She decided to take Sawyer to his room so she wouldn't wake him with her sobs.

I wanted this, she reminded herself.

I could have stayed at Maverick's.

No, she couldn't have. She would have just fallen deeper in love with him every day she was there. This was the smart play.

But man, it sucked.

****

Maverick

He had no desire to go home. Without her and Sawyer there, it was going to be depressingly quiet. So he opted to stop by Flannigan's instead.

The place where it all started.

"Hey, what are you doing here?" Derrick asked when he walked through the door.

"Just thought I'd stop in for dinner and a drink."

His brother furrowed his brows. "Really? Is Olivia meeting you here with my nephew?"

He barked out a mirthless laugh.

"No, I just finished helping her move her things back into her house."

"You did *what*?"

"She's moved out. Our divorce should be finalized in a few weeks.

Derrick set two shot glasses in front of him and filled them with Johnny Walker Blue, then slid one in front of Maverick while tossing the other back himself.

"I hope you got a prenup, brother."

"I did, but I don't give a shit about that. I just want my family."

"So go get them. This isn't like you, to just sit back and not go after what you want."

Maverick shook his head and threw the shot back. "I'd be wasting my time. She's in love with someone else. I thought she'd come around, but it became obvious she was miserable being there. I love her too much to let her be miserable."

"So now you're miserable."

"I'll be okay. She did agree to let me take Sawyer when she's working, so I'll have him a lot."

"That's good. If you need any help with him..."

"I appreciate it."

Derrick lifted the whiskey bottle as if asking if Maverick wanted another.

"No thanks. I'm driving. Plus, I have to pick Sawyer up in the morning."

"Aw man, it's your first night without him? I'm sorry, Mav."

Fuck.

"Maybe I will have one more."

**

Derrick had Dan follow him when he drove Maverick home in the Cullinan.

Mav had argued that he could take an Uber, but his brother replied, "I don't think it's a good idea to leave the Rolls in the parking lot overnight."

"Good point."

The first thing he noticed when they pulled into the garage was her empty parking space.

Derrick must have noticed it, too, because he quietly asked, "You going to be okay? You want me to come in with you?"

He swallowed hard and attempted to smile. "Nah, I'll be okay. Gotta get used to my new normal sometime, right?"

"Yeah, but you don't have to tonight."

"Rip the Band-aid off."

Derrick didn't seem to buy Maverick's brave face act, but the only thing he said was, "If you say so."

He shut the garage door once his brother got into Dan's car and drove away.

Like a glutton for punishment, he walked into the nursery and sat down in the rocking chair, staring at the empty crib.

She should be in here right now, feeding their son and putting him to sleep. And goddammit, she should then be slipping into bed with him, where he'd wrap his arms around her and hold her tight for the next three hours.

He thought about how she'd have that soon enough with Casey. She was going to remarry just like Patricia had, and

Sawyer would have a stepdad, just like Nick and Nash had. And Maverick would be a part-time dad, without a wife or anyone significant in his life, other than his kids.

At least with Sawyer he was going to do the dad thing differently.

He wondered how his boy was doing, and if Olivia was relieved to finally be back in her home.

****

Olivia

Sawyer refused to fall asleep in his new crib, and instead decided to cry inconsolably all night. No matter what she did, he wouldn't stop crying.

It was like he knew she'd taken him from his dad and was punishing her for it.

"Please go to sleep," she begged. "Mommy starts work tomorrow and can't be up all night, Sawyer."

Although in her heart she knew the only way she would get any rest was if she cried herself to sleep. Either way, she was going to need cucumbers for her eyes in the morning. She didn't have cucumbers—she hardly had any groceries, just a barebones delivery to get her through dinner and breakfast.

Ugh, she was going to have to do the grocery shopping again. Maybe Maverick would loan her Juanita. Forget spousal support, just let her have the sweet *abuela* a few days a week.

Even her cats seemed to be mad at her. Oscar was in hiding and Honey threw up next to her food dish to express her displeasure at being back home. Olivia would not be surprised to wake up and find one of them had pooped in her favorite shoes.

"It'll get better," she told herself.

Although she didn't see how. She really wished Maverick were there to come to her rescue.

CHAPTER FORTY-FOUR

Olivia

Maverick was holding her in his arms, stroking her hair and whispering in her ear, "I've got you." A blue unicorn pawed its foot in agreement in the corner, and the baby animals on the wall told her to let Maverick handle everything, so she decided she would.

"Liv, darlin', you need to wake up. You're going to be late."

She jerked her head up with a start. It took her a second to orient herself. Sawyer had finally cried himself into exhaustion around five o'clock, but she was pretty sure she fell asleep before he did, with her head on the crib rail as she sat in the rocking chair listening to him sob.

And Maverick was standing next to her—in the flesh—gently stroking her back.

"Wh—what are you doing here? What time is it?"

She rubbed her eyes, trying to make sense of what was going on.

"You didn't answer the door, so I used the key you gave me. I was going to ask how it went last night, but I think I can guess."

"He wouldn't stop crying. He didn't want to eat, he wouldn't go to sleep... all he would do is cry."

"Do you have patients this morning?"

"No. I was just going to start going through charts and get caught up on paperwork."

"Text Rose and tell her you won't be in until this afternoon. I'll take care of Sawyer. You go get in bed for a few hours."

"No, I can get up."

She rubbed her neck where it had kinked from the way she'd had it resting on the crib rail.

Maverick took over massaging her neck, and she closed her eyes, almost falling asleep in the process.

"I'm sure you can, but I wouldn't trust you to drive. Or prescribe medication to someone."

She felt herself being lifted and the next thing she knew, the comforter was being pulled up around her shoulders. "Go to sleep. I'll text Rose."

CHAPTER FORTY-FIVE

Maverick

Sawyer woke not long after she fell asleep: fussy, hungry, and with green poop.

Obviously keeping his mom awake all night had stressed the little guy out. Fortunately, he was either hungry enough or tired enough to cooperate with Maverick and take a bottle.

Then they had an important discussion about letting his mom sleep at night before he packed the diaper bag, set an alarm on Olivia's phone, and wrote her a quick note, then quietly let himself out.

He needed to create some distance with her, and he knew not being there when she woke up was a good start, otherwise he'd be inclined to try and take care of her. Maybe try to crawl into bed with her.

He sent her a text around one that afternoon.

Maverick: Just checking to make sure your alarm went off and to ask if you want me to keep Sawyer tonight.

She answered right away.

Olivia: It did. Thank you for setting it, that was very thoughtful. And, I decided I'm going to work half days this week, until he gets his schedule figured out. Last night was for the birds.

Maverick: I can only imagine. You were pretty wiped out. That's why I offered to take him.

Olivia: I appreciate it. But, he's going to have to get used to just one of us at night, and the sooner, the better.

Maverick: Speaking of... I would like him a few nights a week. I think the evenings you work late would be best, don't you?

The dots indicating she was replying started and stopped several times. Finally, she sent a response.

Olivia: How many nights are you thinking?

Seven.

Maverick: Two or three.

Olivia: Let's talk when I pick him up this evening?

What was there to talk about? He didn't think two or three nights was unreasonable.

Maverick: Okay. I'll see you later.

Olivia: Around six, okay?

Maverick: I'm flexible. You know that.

**

She rang the doorbell at five minutes after six.

He answered the door with a frown. "Why are you ringing the doorbell, and using the front door? You still have the garage door opener—use it."

"I didn't want to be presumptuous."

"Olivia, you are welcome here anytime."

"Thanks," she said as she stepped inside. "And thank you again for this morning."

"It's going to be an adjustment, but he'll get it figured out."

"How was he today?"

"A little fussy when he first woke up, but after lunch he was his usual, happy self."

"Once he was back here, with you."

Maverick knew that hurt her feelings, so he didn't gloat when he replied, "Yeah."

He didn't expect her to burst into tears, though, but that's exactly what she did. He'd never seen her cry, and it took every ounce of his willpower not to pull her into his arms to try and comfort her.

Instead, he settled for rubbing her biceps. "Hey, it'll be okay. He's just gotta adjust, but kids are resilient. He'll get it figured out."

She wiped her eyes with an embarrassed laugh. "Thanks. I know you're right; I just can't help thinking I'm screwing this up royally and he'll never forgive me."

"You're not screwing this up. You're just exhausted and not thinking straight."

"You're probably right."

"The offer stands; he can stay here tonight so you can get some sleep."

It was on the tip of his tongue to invite her, too, but he bit that appendage and kept his mouth shut.

She replied, "I'm not going in until the afternoon tomorrow, so I'm ready for another sleepless night."

"I'll come by early again unless you text me otherwise."

"Thank you. Maybe he can start staying with you a few nights next week, when I'm back to full-time again."

He really wished she'd slowly ease back into working forty-plus hours, but they were divorcing, and therefore, he didn't get an opinion. Not that he ever had been entitled to one. They'd never been *married* married, as she liked to call it.

Speaking of.

"My lawyer is supposed to get in touch with yours about scheduling a settlement meeting. Just wanted to give you a heads up."

"I already told you, Mav. I don't want your money."

"And I already told you, I want to make sure you have options about working."

Her eyes welled again and big, fat tears rolled down her cheeks when she whispered, "Thanks."

He reached for her, then clenched his fist and brought it down to his side.

"Of course. I've got your back, Liv."

****

Olivia

Whoever he did fall in love with someday was going to be a lucky woman.

Ugh. And she was going to be Sawyer's stepmom.

Olivia hated her already.

CHAPTER FORTY-SIX

Olivia

It took the rest of the week, but Sawyer did eventually settle into his new routine. Maverick had been a godsend, showing up early in the morning so she could finally get some sleep.

On Saturday, her day off, he still showed up early in the morning. "I'll take him today so you can rest and get caught up with laundry, or whatever else you need to do."

Olivia wanted to ask why he was so good to her, but she already knew the answer. She was sure he was probably just as good to Patricia, although she'd yet to meet his ex-wife.

Monday, her first official full day back, she had patients scheduled and quickly fell behind, so she was late picking Sawyer up from Maverick's.

As she leaned down to collect the diaper bag, her stomach growled loudly.

Embarrassed, she said, "Sorry. I didn't get a chance to grab lunch from the cafeteria today."

"Do you have food at home?"

No. Well, cereal.

"Oh, yeah."

He raised an eyebrow at her. "When did that happen?"

"I have food," she replied defensively.

"Take some enchiladas. Juanita made them today."

Her stomach rumbled at the thought of his housekeeper's delicious cooking.

She was starving, so that beat out her pride. "That sounds great. Thank you."

The next morning, when she went through the kitchen on her way to the garage, she discovered a brown paper sack on the counter with her name on it.

She opened it up to find a sandwich in a sealed plastic bag, granola bar and fruit cup complete with a spoon, and a brownie wrapped in plastic wrap.

He'd made her lunch.

His third wife was one lucky bitch.

**

Amy, her nurse practitioner, poked her head around the doorway to Olivia's office on Thursday.

"We're going to grab a drink if you want to come."

She really didn't, but Sawyer was staying with Maverick for the first time, and she knew she was going to be a wreck all night at home by herself. Going out with the girls seemed a better alternative to pacing her halls.

Shutting her computer down, she rolled her chair from her desk.

"Sure, that sounds fun."

"Julie is driving so we can leave our cars in the hospital garage and not have to worry about getting them tomorrow since they'll already be at work. That way we just have to Uber home tonight and to work tomorrow."

"You guys think of everything," Olivia teased with a smile as she pulled her purse and coat from her closet.

She sat in the back of her office manager's minivan and listened while the nurses and staff caught her up on three months of gossip.

It wasn't until the van stopped that she noticed where they were.

Oh no.

"You guys like Flannigan's?"

"Oh yeah," Amy answered. "They have the best fries, and their Thursday night drink specials are cheap. Plus, their bartenders are hot."

Olivia put her game face on. "Can't argue with that logic."

Maybe she could hide in a corner booth and no one she knew would recognize her.

There was no way she could be that lucky, because who approached their table? None other than Derrick himself.

She should have known—a table full of beautiful women? Of course he was going to wait on them.

"Ladies," he said with his famous Mitchell smile. "What are you celebrating tonight?"

The women giggled, and Julie replied, "Nothing, we're just getting off of work."

Janice added, "And Flannigan's has the best fries and drink specials."

Olivia could tell that was exactly what Derrick wanted to hear.

Meanwhile, Amy twirled her hair and corrected her friends. "Actually, we are celebrating!" She pointed directly at Olivia. "Dr. Lacroix has finally returned to work after three months of maternity leave."

Shit. Shit. Shit.

So much for staying invisible.

Derrick's smile fell when they locked eyes, and he lifted his chin in greeting. "Olivia."

She mirrored the gesture. "Derrick."

"You know Dr. Lacroix?" Amy asked.

Derrick kept his eyes trained on Olivia. "She's my sister-in-law." He arrogantly raised his eyebrows. "Where's Sawyer?"

The asshole knew damn well where her son was.

"Mav has him tonight."

Meanwhile, she felt her staff's eyes lobbing back and forth between them.

"You know, you're the only woman my brother—"

She interrupted him while he was in mid-sentence, getting out of the booth and grabbing his arm to lead him away from the table

"Do you mind? Those women work for me. I'd prefer not to air my dirty laundry in front of them."

"I was only going to say, you're the only woman who ever managed to break my brother's heart."

"Oh, you're right," she snarked as she rolled her eyes. "That's not fodder for office gossip."

Then what he said sank in, and she defensively crossed her arms in front of her chest. "And Maverick is hardly heartbroken. He got what he wanted. Sawyer is with him more than half the time."

"He wants you, too. He's crazy about you."

Olivia jerked her head back. "No, he's not."

"Um, I've known Pete my whole life, and I can say with one hundred percent certainty that he is head over heels in love with you."

"He's in love with his son."

"Yeah, and his son's mother."

Derrick's words made her heart drop to her stomach. If this was some kind of joke, it was just mean.

"Why would you say that?"

"Other than I have eyes and have seen the way you two look at each other? He told me."

Maverick told him? She was dying to ask what exactly he said, but it felt too high school-ish.

Derrick continued with his truth bombs. "And I'd be willing to bet you love him, too."

"How do you—?"

"Like I said, I have eyes, Olivia. The only person you're fooling is yourself. Well, and apparently my brother. For two people who otherwise seem pretty smart, you two are morons when it comes to each other."

She stared dumbstruck at Derrick, while he seemed rather pleased with himself.

He jerked his head toward her table and said, "Tell your friends I'll be right back to get their drink order," and he turned and walked away like he'd just dropped the mic.

Olivia was in a fog the rest of the night, and the next day passed in a blur.

She debated what she was going to say to Maverick when she picked Sawyer up after work. By the time she was in her Mercedes on her way to his house, she'd convinced herself that Derrick was wrong.

Yes, Maverick *cared* about her—she was the mother of his infant son—but he wasn't *in love* with her. He would have told her if he was.

Like you told him?

Hey, inner voice—we're talking about him, not me. Put a sock in it.

She noticed Nick's truck in the driveway when she pulled up to Maverick's house, and when she opened the garage door, the Cullinan was gone.

Weird.

"Hello?" she called out when she walked into the kitchen.

She heard Nick's voice call from the family room, "In here!"

She found Sawyer and Nick on a quilt on the floor, with toys and books strewn everywhere.

"Hey!" the older Mitchell boy called enthusiastically. "Dad had to run some errands, so he asked me to stay with Sawyer until you got here."

"Everything go okay?"

"Oh yeah. Me and my little bro have just been hanging out, and he's been telling me all kinds of stories." Nick tickled Sawyer's belly, asking, "Right little dude?" as the baby squealed and kicked in response.

Her son's happiness made her smile as she started picking up the mess of toys.

"Oh, just leave those. I'll take care of them," Nick said. "Dad told me to tell you to call him if you want him to pick up Sawyer tomorrow, and to make sure you take the dinner he put aside for you in the fridge."

She appreciated Mav's thoughtfulness, still she said, "Aw he shouldn't have," as she picked up Sawyer from the quilt.

Nick stood and handed her the diaper bag. "You know dad."

When they reached the kitchen Nick opened the fridge and pulled out the plastic container with the dinner.

"He really loves you, you know," he said as he handed it to her.

"Why do you say that?"

He motioned to the container of food in her hand. "He takes care of the people he loves."

"He wants to make sure Sawyer is getting the proper nutrition."

"He worries about *you*. Because he loves you."

Could that really be true? Had she been so blind that she'd missed it?

****

Maverick

He sat across from his attorney and looked at the million-dollar view from the man's office. Their divorce negotiation with Olivia and her lawyer was in less than half an hour, and they were hammering out the details before the meeting.

If everything went according to plan today, the only thing left to do would be to appear before a judge and ask him to grant them their divorce.

"Her two million dollars is non-negotiable, unless she wants more—then give it to her. Spousal maintenance and child support is also not up for debate—unless again, if she asks for more, then she can have it."

"So, you want to fight about making her *take* your money?"

"Yes."

"And you think that's going to be a sticking point?"

"Yes."

"What about custody?"

"I think we're on the same page when it comes to that. I'll provide Sawyer's care while she's at work, and he'll stay with me two nights a week, more if she needs it. She'll have him on her days off."

"What about holidays? And when he starts school?"

"He'll go to the school in my district, and holidays... I'd prefer we spend them together."

Larry shook his head. "Trust me, we need to spell out what will happen when either, or both of you, gets remarried."

Maverick couldn't help snapping, "Then I guess she brings her new husband along if he feels he needs to be included."

With a gentler tone, his lawyer asked, "And what about you, when you get involved with someone new?"

"I don't see that happening."

"No, not now. But trust me, I've been doing this a long time. You will. Someday."

He doubted it.

"Look, Patricia and I made it work when she married Ken. We spent the major holidays and boys' birthdays together."

"The kids' birthdays, yes, but then when they got older you started alternating holidays."

The whole premise of this was pissing him off.

"Fine," he snarled. "When he's ten, we can alternate holidays if that's something she decides she wants to do."

Larry made a few notes, then closed his leather portfolio. "We've covered the major points. I think we're ready."

Whoopee.

"Can I go then? My secretary is watching Sawyer, and I want to get back to the office."

"Sure. Just keep your phone handy in case there's a problem."

Maverick couldn't imagine there would be a problem, but agreed to be available if needed. Then he stormed out of the office, running into his gorgeous, soon-to-be ex-wife on his way to the elevator. She looked beautiful, as always, dressed in a lime green and black silk blouse, black pencil skirt with a slit up the side, and black strappy heels.

"Are you leaving?" she asked.

"Yeah, I've told my attorney my non-negotiables. You and I have discussed them, so you already know what they are."

"I think you should stay for this meeting. I added a few things we hadn't discussed and they might be sticking points for you."

He felt his blood pressure spike.

"Why would you do that, Olivia? I thought we had a deal."

She shrugged. "I decided these were important."

"If it's about money, I don't care. Larry already knows you can have however much you want."

She shook her head. "It's about custody."

Oh fuck no.

He felt she'd just stabbed him in the back. They had an arrangement, dammit.

"Just come back and hear what I'm proposing," she pleaded. "You might be okay with it."

"I doubt that," he growled as they headed toward the conference room.

He sat on the opposite side of the conference table next to his attorney and tried to contain his scowl as her attorney presented two folders and opened them before sliding them across the wooden surface. One in front of Maverick, the other in front of Larry.

"We looked over the terms that Mr. Nielsen sent over, and Olivia wanted to make some changes. You'll see them outlined in the documents in front of you."

"What kind of changes?" Larry asked suspiciously before glancing down at the paperwork.

Maverick was already looking at the changes she wanted. The words on the paper didn't make sense.

He glanced up at Olivia. "You're agreeing to give me full custody on the condition that you move back into my house?"

"Well, it's more specific than that," she said softly.

He kept reading. "And into the owner's bedroom?"

She nodded.

Confused, but hopeful, he asked, "I don't understand Olivia."

"I want to be *married* married to you, Pete."

Her attorney stood and said to Larry, "Maybe we need to give these two a minute."

Larry remained seated but turned to Maverick.

"Mav?"

"Yeah. Let me talk to my wife in private, please."

****

Olivia

Once the lawyers left the room, he came around the table and grabbed her hand.

"You want to be *married* married? To me?"

"You are my husband."

"But I've been your husband for almost three months. Why now?"

She answered his question with a question.

"Do you love me? Not as the mother of your children, like you do Patricia. But as your wife—someone you want to fall asleep next to—naked—every night, and wake up next to every day for the rest of your life?"

"Isn't it obvious?"

"No, Mav, it's not."

He cupped her face in his hands and stared into her eyes.

"I am so in love with you, Olivia Lacroix, it makes my chest ache. Your beauty, your brains, your body... what an amazing mother you are—what an amazing *woman* you are. All of it."

Her heart was racing so fast she felt dizzy.

"Why didn't you ever say anything?"

"You're in love with someone else. I thought if I showed you, maybe you'd grow to love me, but..."

She interrupted him, blurting out, "I love you, Pete Mitchell."

He searched her eyes. "You do?"

She nodded her head, whispering, "So much."

He stared at her for another beat before capturing her lips with his. He kissed her like she was his oxygen supply while she clung to his shirt.

All the pain and sadness she'd been harboring suddenly vanished as his tongue explored her mouth, demanding her submission, which she eagerly gave him. He made her feel desired and safe.

Maverick pushed her skirt to her waist and lifted her onto the end of the table, his mouth never leaving hers as he slid her panties to the side and ran a finger down her slit. She knew she was wet—her deprived pussy needed to be filled.

Reaching for his cock, she found him hard as a rock under his pants.

"Mav," she whispered as she broke their kiss. "Please..." She didn't care they were in his attorney's conference room.

Apparently, neither did he, because he lowered his zipper, pulled his cock out, and thrust inside her, smothering her moan with his mouth.

No words were spoken as he filled her, balls deep. This exchange was carnal, Maverick needing to brand her with his cum in her womb, and Olivia needing to be marked.

She wrapped her legs around his back, and he stroked her clit with his fingers as he thrust his cock in deeper.

"I love you so much," he moaned with his face buried in her neck while he filled her over and over.

"I love you, too, my husband."

He lifted his head and held her hips. "God, I love the sound of that."

"I love saying it."

"I'm not letting you go, darlin'," he warned, picking up speed.

"Don't ever let me go," she begged. Her orgasm started to creep into her belly.

"You're mine. Forever."

"Yes, forever," she panted as her body went taut while she teetered on the edge of her climax.

"Tell me again," he demanded, his finger moving at a furious pace over her clit.

"I love you, husband."

"Fuuuuuuck!" he whisper-roared as he pulled her hips tight against his. She could feel the ropes of cum hitting her walls, and that set off her own orgasm.

Maverick planted his mouth on hers to stifle her cries, and she clung to him as her body shuddered in ecstasy.

Finally, he dropped his forehead to hers.

"You want to move home?"

"I never wanted to leave."

He closed his eyes and groaned, "Then why did you?"

"I thought you only wanted to be with me because of Sawyer."

He pulled his cock out and handed her the box of tissues that was on the table.

"No, sweetheart. I love you both, but I thought you couldn't wait to divorce me so you could be with Casey."

She tossed the tissues into the trash and pulled her skirt down once she hopped off the table. "Can I tell you a secret?"

He cocked his head suspiciously as he tucked himself into his pants. "I don't know...?"

"Casey is my ex. But we'd been broken up for almost a year before I met you and got pregnant."

"So, this whole time... you never had a boyfriend?"

"No."

"All that, if you'd only waited a few months, you could have had the love of your life's baby..."

"It wasn't true. I was protecting myself because *you* are the love of my life, but I didn't think you felt the same way."

He grabbed her face and kissed her again. "How could you not know? I tried to show you every day."

"I thought because I was Sawyer's mom..."

"I don't worship Patricia, and she's the mother of two of my sons."

"She's also married to someone else," she replied dismissively, then added, "And you *worship* me?"

"The fucking ground you walk on. I plan on taking you home and showing you just how much."

They walked out of the conference room hand in hand, and Maverick announced, "Gentlemen, your services are no longer needed."

Both attorneys smiled, and Larry said, "I figured as much."

CHAPTER FORTY-SEVEN

Maverick

"Hey Pam," he said into the cabin of the Rolls. "How's Sawyer? Everything okay?"

"The little angel is sleeping right now. He took a bottle, had his diaper changed, and fell asleep in my arms."

He looked over at Olivia in the passenger seat and smiled as he reached for her hand and squeezed.

"You're not still holding him, are you?"

"Maybe I am, maybe I'm not. Don't worry about it."

He laughed, then asked, "Is it okay if I'm a little later than I thought?"

"If you're not here by five, he'll just come home with Auntie Pam."

"I'll be there before then. I'm just taking a long lunch."

"Take as long you need. We're all good here."

Maverick ended the call, then asked, "Do you need to phone your office?"

"I already told them I wasn't coming back."

"You were that confident, huh?"

"After what Derrick and Nick told me, I was that *hopeful.* Plus, I decided if it didn't end well, it was probably a good idea not to go back to work, anyway."

He glanced over at her as he turned the wheel into his neighborhood.

"What Derrick and Nick told you?"

"They both said you were in love with me, and that basically I was an idiot for not seeing it."

"Well... they weren't wrong."

She playfully slugged his arm. "Hey!"

Maverick held his hand up defensively and laughed. "About me being in love with you!"

"They were right. I was an idiot," she admitted. "I just didn't want to be vulnerable."

"We both were idiots. Being vulnerable is scary."

"Not being with you because I was too proud to tell you is even scarier."

He kissed her ringless left ring finger. "I promise to always be honest with you about what I'm feeling from now on, but you have to promise to do the same."

"I promise."

"Good. So what I'm feeling right now is that I really want to take you home and take my time making love to you. Then I want to go back to your old house and pack your things, put your wedding and engagement rings back on, and take you back home so I can make love to you again while I look at my ring on your hand. Then, I want you to take the rest of the week off work so we can spend the entire time in bed whispering how much we love each other. Then, while our son naps, we'll have hot sex."

"I definitely want you to take me home and make love to me, but I have another confession to make."

"Oh boy. Am I going to hate this one?"

"I hope not." She sat up on her knees in the passenger seat and leaned over the console to whisper in his ear. "I really liked it when you punished me for messing with your tools."

The corner of his mouth lifted. "Darlin', I will happily punish you any time you want, if you promise to never—ever—touch my tools again."

"That's not a euphemism, right?"

"No. I want you to touch *that* tool. But no more not saying exactly what we mean. From now on, my tools are the ones in my garage, working out is really exercising—like lifting weights or doing cardio. And if I want to fuck you senseless, I'll just let you know."

"Or you can just throw me over your shoulder and take me..."

He *knew* she'd liked that.

So when they pulled into the garage, he did exactly that, and marched straight to their bedroom, where he set her gently down on the bed and unfastened the buttons on her blouse.

"I'm not going to rip your clothes this time, sweetheart, since you don't have any here. Plus, I was serious when I said I want to make love to you. I don't want to make *like*, and pull your hair as I fuck you hard." He was throwing her words back at her. "I'm going to take my time and worship your body how I want. How you deserve."

She let out a small gasp. "Oh!"

He tugged her hair playfully, so she had no choice but to look up at him. "Then I'm going to fuck you hard and pull your hair."

She smiled when his lips captured hers, and she wrapped her arms around his neck, holding him closer as their kisses grew more frenzied. When he buried his face in her neck, she murmured, "Anything you say, Mr. Mitchell."

He pulled back and looked down at her with a smug grin. "And that's another thing, *Dr. Mitchell.*"

"What if I hyphenate my name, at least professionally?"

"You don't expect me to hyphenate mine, do you?"

"That's a pretty sexist attitude, if you expect me to change my name but won't change yours."

His shoulders fell in defeat. He was about to tell her he'd change his name to whatever she wanted as long as she stayed married to him when she grinned and pulled him closer to whisper in his ear, "I'm just teasing."

"Thank fuck." He sighed with relief.

"But you probably should make love to me now and seal the deal before I change my mind."

EPILOGUE

Maverick

They walked out of the courthouse, paperwork for Olivia's name change in one hand while she held Maverick's hand with the other.

"So, Dr. Mitchell, I just texted Yvette and Hope and told them we're on our way."

She'd decided to make her maiden name one of her middle names and go by Dr. Olivia Lacroix Mitchell professionally for a while.

"Is it gauche to have another wedding ceremony not even six months after our first?"

"No! Our friends are excited for us and want to share in our happiness."

She looked at him skeptically. "Or enjoy the open bar and the June weather at the Cape."

"Eh, that too."

"Couldn't we have just had a party?"

"No way. I want attendants, sappy vows, our first dance, tossing of the garter and bouquet, tears of joy... the whole nine yards this time."

"You kind of sound like a girl," she teased as he opened the passenger door for her.

"I don't care. I'm perfectly content with my masculinity. And you didn't have any complaints about it this morning in the shower," he countered just before he shut the car door.

"No, I didn't," she told him with a satisfied smile when he got in the driver's side. "I love when you remind me you're the boss."

He leaned over and pecked her lips. "I love that you let me be the boss."

****

Olivia

She knew he was kidding. Pete 'Maverick' Mitchell didn't need anyone's permission for anything. But she loved that when it came to his family, he was a giant teddy bear. Especially with her.

"It looks like the weather is going to cooperate," he told her as he eased the SUV onto the road.

"That's good. Taylor was worried how we were going to fit one hundred people into the B & B if it rained."

He threw his favorite mantra at her. "We would have made it work."

She didn't mind it so much now. Actually, she found it comforting, because she knew she could count on him to do just that.

He'd originally wanted to rent a ballroom and have five hundred people at this wedding. Fortunately, Olivia had been able to rein him in, with the help of Evan's girlfriend, Hope. She and Yvette, Hope's best friend from San Diego, owned a bed and breakfast on the Cape and offered to rent them the entire property for the weekend. Luckily, the Dragonfly Inn couldn't accommodate any more than one hundred people on the property.

Yvette and James Rudolf, a doctor who also worked at Boston General, just had a baby girl of their own in March, so she had been spending most of her time in the city. And Hope's job in the lab at Boston General kept her busy. But the two women had an excellent staff. Taylor, a recent college graduate had been really helpful with all the wedding preparations, while Isaac, the resident handyman, promised he could bring all the preparations to life.

Taylor met them in the front lobby.

"Welcome to the Dragonfly Inn! Your parents just got here about an hour ago with your son. I've gotten them situated in their room, and Isaac will show you to the bridal suite."

Isaac was much younger than Olivia had been expecting. And the longing smile he gave Taylor when he walked by her at the front desk had Olivia wondering if there was more to their story than just handyman and guest relations manager.

She kind of hoped so. She wanted everyone to be happy and in love like she was.

****

Maverick

Two days later, his breath caught in his chest when he saw his wife standing at the end of the aisle in the bed and breakfast's garden in her white sleeveless wedding dress. The plunging V-neckline and tight, jeweled bodice made her boobs look fucking amazing. While the lacy skirt and short train circling her feet made her look elegant as she made her way along the white runner leading to him.

It seemed like it took her forever to reach him, and when he finally took her hand, it was like he could breathe again.

"You are absolutely stunning," he whispered in her ear before they turned and walked up the small steps of the gazebo together to the waiting pastor.

With Nick and Nash at his side, and Rose and Evan next to her, it felt like the perfect day. Even her twin smiled when Olivia held her hand entwined with Maverick's up in victory when they were presented to the crowd as husband and wife—again.

At the reception, Olivia brought over a baby girl to the table where Maverick was holding Sawyer.

"Who's that?" he asked his bride.

"This is Sawyer's future girlfriend, Abby. Her mom is one of the owners of The Dragonfly Inn, and her dad's an anesthesiologist at Boston General with me."

Their six-month old son was fascinated with the little girl.

Abby, who was just barely three months, wasn't as aware of her surroundings as their little boy, and wasn't nearly as impressed with him.

"Just be patient, buddy," Maverick advised him with a knowing smile. "The good ones are worth the wait.

Olivia reached over and softly kissed his lips. "I couldn't agree more."

****

Olivia

"And this is Aiden Matthews; he also works with me," she told her husband as they walked around to mingle with their guests. "He's the guy to call if your heart stops working."

"Sounds like someone I definitely should know," Maverick said with a chuckle as he shook the cardiologist's hand.

Aiden smiled back—a rare occurrence for him since his ugly divorce a few years ago. While the salty doctor could physically fix your heart if it stopped working, apparently he wasn't able to repair his broken one.

"Congratulations," he offered.

Olivia was dying to ask what happened with Dakota, the hippy chick he'd met at Steven's house on the Cape last summer. Aiden had responded with her name as his 'plus one' on the RSVP card, however, she'd been nowhere to be found that night.

But she knew better than to pry into Aiden's life. He played everything close to the vest and had no problem telling people to mind their own business—usually not delicately, either.

With a smile, she closed her hand around her husband's. She was so lucky to have found him. She wished that for her friend.

She used to think she'd spend her life as a single mom, and here she was, married to the love of her life with a beautiful baby boy.

Miracles really could happen.

****

Get Aiden and Dakota's story in *Wicked Hot Heart Doc!* Coming in 2023!

Want to read about the other couples in the series?
Hope and Evan—*Wicked Hot Medicine*
https://tesssummersauthor.com/wicked-hot-medicine
Steven and Whitney—*Wicked Hot Doctor*
https://tesssummersauthor.com/wicked-hot-doctor-1
James and Yvette—*Wicked Hot Baby Daddy*
https://tesssummersauthor.com/wicked-hot-baby-daddy-1
Zach and Zoe—*Wicked Bad Decisions*
https://tesssummersauthor.com/wicked-bad-decisions-1
Parker and Xandra—*Wicked Hot Silver Fox*
https://tesssummersauthor.com/wicked-hot-silver-fox-1

THANK YOU

Thank you for reading *Wicked Little Secret!*

I came up with the premise of Nick, Maverick's son, being the one to drive Olivia to the hospital while she was in labor on one of my morning walks, and the story snowballed from there!

Although, my characters stopped talking to me for a while, as they typically do when I'm on deadline. They're worse than children sometimes!

If you enjoyed the book (and even if you didn't), would you mind leaving me a review wherever you purchased this book? And, if it's not too much trouble, Goodreads and/or Bookbub? Your review helps get my book seen by other readers, which lets me keep writing, so I would be grateful for anything you can do!

Don't forget to sign up for my newsletter to get a free full-size novel, bonus content, and be the first to know about cover reveals, contests, excerpts, and more!

https://www.subscribepage.com/TessSummersNewsletter

xoxo,

Tess

ACKNOWLEDGMENTS

To my family: I owe you a big thank you for being so patient while I finished this book when we were on vacation. You guys are awesome, and I hope you still had a good time.

Eden Bradley: Wow, did I make you work on this one. I'm sorry. Thank you for your patience and encouragement, and for just making this book better. And for not firing me.

OliviaProDesigns: Another great cover. Thank you.

Anna Lena Milo: I appreciate all the help you give me every day.

To my readers: I am grateful you love my stories and characters and continue to want to read my books. I am the luckiest person in the world that I get to do what I do every day. Thank you from the bottom of my heart.

Lastly, to Mr. Summers: Thank you for continuing to support me on this crazy journey. I couldn't do it without you. I promise on our next Puerto Vallarta trip I will not be on deadline, and you will have all my attention!

Wicked Bad Decisions

Don't hate the player, hate the game.
But what happens when the rules of the game change?

Attorney Zach Rudolf gave up on love the day his girlfriend dumped him for someone who could give her children. Fortunately for Zach, being rich and handsome has its advantages. It wasn't hard to find women—yes, plural—to replace her and help lick... his wounds.

Then he meets *her*. The woman he'd change his ways for and settle down.

Feisty, beautiful, and rich, Zoe has also had her share of heartbreak, which is why she's perfected the art cougaring. (It's a verb, just ask her.) This means Zach's age puts him firmly in the friend-zone.

Something Zach finds completely agonizing and totally unacceptable. And he's going to show her just how unacceptable he thinks it is.

https://tesssummersauthor.com/wicked-bad-decisions-1

Wicked Hot Baby Daddy

The player doctor left behind more than a broken heart.

Dr. James Rudolf made Yvette Sinclair believe in fairy tales, and he was her Prince Charming. Then, out of the blue, he stopped taking her calls. Blocked them would be a more accurate descriptor.

Devastated, Yvette had no idea why the man she thought was *the one* had ghosted her. Even harder, she was three thousand miles away, so she couldn't just show up at his house and demand an explanation. Then her best friend started seeing him around Boston—a different beautiful woman on his arm each time. She felt like such a fool.

She was determined to move on and forget all about the playboy. Until two pink lines made that impossible.

Get it here! https://tesssummersauthor.com/wicked-hot-baby-daddy-1

Wicked Hot Medicine

Vengeance never tasted as sweet as it did on Hope Ericson's skin.

Sleeping with his rival's wife was an opportunity Dr. Evan Lacroix couldn't refuse.

Except, it turned out, she wasn't his wife—she was his sister.

Oh, the irony. It made it that much sweeter.

Unfortunately, when Hope realized his intentions, she didn't appreciate being a pawn in his game, and the sassy spitfire turned the tables on him.

Evan never saw it coming.

And now he needs to decide which is more important— love or revenge.

This isn't a book about enemies *to* lovers. It's about enemies with benefits—until the line between enemy and lover gets blurred.

https://tesssummersauthor.com/wicked-hot-medicine

Wicked Hot Doctor

A single doctor and a single lawyer walk into a bar...

Dr. Steven Ericson never thought a parking ticket would change his life, but that's exactly what happened the day he goes downtown to pay his forgotten ticket for an expired meter.

As the head of Boston General's ER, he doesn't have time for relationships, or at least he's never met a woman who made him want to make time.

That all changes when he meets Whitney Hayes. The dynamo attorney in high heels entices him to imagine carving out time for more than his usual one-night stand. Imagine his dismay to find out that she, too, doesn't do relationships— they're not in her 5-year plan.

Yeah, eff that. Her plan needs rewriting, and Steven's more than willing to supply the pen and ink to help with that.

https://tesssummersauthor.com/wicked-hot-doctor-1

Wicked Hot Silver Fox

It all started with a dirty photo in his text messages…

Yeah, Dr. Parker Preston's intentions when he gave Alexandra Collins his phone number at the animal rescue gala were more personal than professional. But he'd never expected the sassy beauty with the blue streak in her hair to send him a picture of her perfect, perky boobs as enticement to adopt the dogs she was desperately trying to find a home for.

But dang if they weren't the ideal incentive for him to offer his home to more than just the dogs. In exchange for adopting the older, bonded pair, she'd need to move in with him for a month and get the dogs acclimated. Oh, and she wouldn't be sleeping in the guest room during her stay.

The deal is only for a month though. And she insisted they weren't going to fall in love, something he readily agreed with. They had the rules in place, what could possibly go wrong in four short weeks?

Get it here! https://tesssummersauthor.com/wicked-hot-silver-fox-1

SAN DIEGO SOCIAL SCENE

Operation Sex Kitten: (Ava and Travis)
　https://books2read.com/u/3yzyG6?affiliate=off
The General's Desire: (Brenna and Ron)
　https://books2read.com/u/m2Mpek?affiliate=off
Playing Dirty: (Cassie and Luke)
　https://books2read.com/u/3RNEdj?affiliate=off
Cinderella and the Marine: (Cooper and Katie)
　https://books2read.com/u/3LYenM?affiliate=off
The Heiress and the Mechanic: (Harper and Ben)
　https://books2read.com/u/bQVEn6?affiliate=off
Burning Her Resolve: (Grace and Ryan)
　https://books2read.com/u/bzoEXz?affiliate=off
This Is It: (Paige and Grant)
　https://books2read.com/ThisIsIt?affiliate=off

AGENTS OF ENSENADA

Ignition: (Kennedy and Dante prequel)
https://tesssummersauthor.com/ignition-1
Inferno: (Kennedy and Dante)
https://books2read.com/u/bpaYGJ?affiliate=off
Combustion: (Reagan and Mason)
https://books2read.com/u/baaME6?affiliate=off
Reignited: (Taren and Jacob)
https://books2read.com/u/3ya2Jl?affiliate=off
Flashpoint: (Sophia and Ramon)
https://books2read.com/TessSummersFlashpoint?affiliate=off

ABOUT THE AUTHOR

Tess Summers is a former businesswoman and teacher who always loved writing but never seemed to have time to sit down and write a short story, let alone a novel. Now battling MS, her life changed dramatically, and she has finally slowed down enough to start writing all the stories she's been wanting to tell, including the fun and sexy ones!

Married over twenty-six years with three grown children, Tess is a former dog foster mom who ended up failing and adopting them instead. She and her husband (and their three dogs) split their time between the desert of Arizona and the lakes of Michigan, so she's always in a climate that's not too hot and not too cold, but just right!

CONTACT ME!

Sign up for my newsletter: BookHip.com/SNGBXD
Email: TessSummersAuthor@yahoo.com
Visit my website: www.TessSummersAuthor.com
Facebook: http://facebook.com/TessSummersAuthor
My FB Group: Tess Summers Sizzling Playhouse
TikTok: https://www.tiktok.com/@tesssummersauthor
Instagram: https://www.instagram.com/tesssummers/
Amazon: https://amzn.to/2MHHhdK
BookBub https://www.bookbub.com/profile/tess-summers
Goodreads - https://www.goodreads.com/TessSummers
Twitter: http://twitter.com/@mmmTess